SOMEONE ELSE'S SHOES

Caela Anne Provost

"You never really understand a person until you consider things from his point of view – until you climb into his skin and walk around in it."

- spoken by Atticus Finch in *To Kill a Mockingbird* by Harper Lee

ISBN: 1539848396
ISBN 13: 9781539848394
Library of Congress Control Number: 2016918255
CreateSpace Independent Publishing Platform
North Charleston, South Carolina

-To my dearest, most wonderful Auntie Lynn: my biggest fan and the person who inspired my love of writing and literature in the first place.

-To Dr. Donald Anderson, for seeing this project through from its beginnings in Fontaine Hall, to its culmination, and for encouraging me to believe in the power of my own unique voice.

PROLOGUE

Vera raced through the darkened corridors of the school constantly looking over her shoulder, hoping to lose the person rapidly pursuing her. She could still hear him behind her—his heavy breathing and his angry screams. In desperation, Vera called out to Atticus, hoping he would come to help her even though she knew he was too far away to hear her. Why did she say she didn't need him? She needed Atticus; he was everything to her...how could she just push him away?

Seeing no other way out, Vera ran for the art room; she couldn't outrun him forever, but maybe she could hide long enough to plan an escape and go to the police. Vera spotted the tall art cabinet in the corner of the room; it wasn't the best hiding place, but it was all she could think of with the time she had. As soon as she settled herself into the cabinet, she could hear heavy footsteps approach the door.

Vera held her breath and cupped her hands over her mouth, fingernails digging into her cheek. The footsteps were in the room now, and they were coming towards her hiding place. Vera began to cry silently. If he found her, he would surely kill her... she knew too much... and then she would never be able to see her family and friends again. She would never get the chance to tell Atticus how much he meant to her.

Suddenly the breathing became louder and the footsteps stopped...right in front of the cabinet. Vera braced herself as the cabinet doors were forced open. She sat speechless as the shadow in front of her said, "Vera Walker, did you really think I wouldn't find you?"

CHAPTER ONE

"Big day tomorrow," said Atticus, feeling compelled to break the silence between himself and his seemingly upset best friend. Atticus absolutely loathed prolonged silence.

"It's really no big deal, Finch… it's a sixteenth birthday. It's not like I'm getting married or winning the Pulitzer Prize." Vera Walker was many things: intelligent, driven, and unfailingly kind. An old soul of sorts, Vera didn't pay much heed to fitting in to what others felt was the stereotypical way to look or behave. She didn't look like a model, and she was fine with that. Vera was strong, and her beauty was most noticeable to those around her when they took the time to talk to her. Vera's modesty and compassion made her peers feel at ease, and her natural inner and outer beauty drew everyone to her like wild hummingbirds to nectar. Yet even though she was well-liked, she did not enjoy being the center of attention-a trait which made her quite the anomaly at her high school. Then again, not even Vera understood herself completely, so she never blamed those around her that questioned as well.

Having a huge sixteenth birthday party would provide Vera with nothing that she wanted. She didn't need to be showered with gifts and she absolutely didn't want any extra attention. Plus, her birthday always reminded her of her parents, her real parents, the ones she would never meet, never understand, and never know. She had come to accept the death of her parents, and she loved the people who adopted her as a baby, but that didn't change how she felt about her birthday. In actuality, Vera would have preferred her parents celebrating her adoption day instead…what good was a birthday if no one around you was there for your first one?

"It may not be a big deal to you, Ver, but I can assure you that it's a big deal to other people. I don't think you understand how many people in this school would kill to be me…everyone wants to be your friend, Ver, everyone expects you to have, well, a party."

"That's all very nice, Finch—"

"*Please*, stop calling me that…"

"*Fine.* That's all very nice, Att-i-cus, but you know that my perfect birthday celebration consists of you and me going to the ice cream stand after school, renting a really good scary movie from the place downtown- if possible one without a ton a gross of torture scenes-, having cake with my family, and spending the rest of the night watching the movie and just talking. You've known me since pre-school. You know the drill."

"Alright, alright," Atticus said grinning, "I'm not saying I want to break tradition, Ver. All I'm saying is that all feelings you have personally about your birthday aside, people care about you, Vera. I care that you're turning Sweet Sixteen… and I'm only a little jealous that you're doing so a month before me."

"A little? Finch, you won't drop the subject."

"Fine…maybe a lot jealous. Happy?"

Vera looked at Atticus Wells, studying his expression. She could tell that he meant it when he said he cared about her. His eyes were so sincere and their warm hazel color went perfectly with his dark brown hair. Atticus was tall, but not intimidating. He was uniquely handsome- Vera always described him as a "Peter Parker" type, a description that Atticus always scoffed at saying that he wasn't nearly as brilliant at Peter. Regardless, Vera felt very safe with him. It was this feeling of safety that had drawn her to Atticus in the first place.

"Yes...thank you," Vera said with a smirk in the direction of her best friend.

"You're very welcome," Atticus replied while looking down at the most wonderful, most stunning girl he had ever met. In all his almost sixteen years, Atticus had never met a girl quite like Vera. Her eyes were the brightest blue he had ever seen and her long light brown hair always seemed to fall in the right place. She was medium height, with a thin-athletic build, and when she walked she seemed to glide.

But if you asked Atticus why he liked her, he would tell you in one word... she's truly *beautiful*. And for Atticus, this didn't just mean she was hot, pretty, or attractive. To him, Vera was beautiful inside and out... he would do anything for her.

A booming voice suddenly interrupted Atticus's thoughts and made him jump.

"Vera Walker," said Principal McCormac, nearly shouting at the girl. "How's Arcadia High School's brightest student doing? I hear someone has a birthday coming up!"

Vera and Atticus had been under the "control" of Principal McCormac since middle school. He was known to all the students as "a man whose voice matched his build." He definitely wasn't a man who was easy to contend with physically or intellectually. Arcadia High School was very lucky to have him, so the students were incessantly told, as he was a decorated writer of a number excellent essay pieces. Neither Vera nor Atticus cared for him very much as they didn't appreciate the devout love he had for himself, but this fact didn't deter either of them from responding politely to their principal.

"I'm well, thank you, sir," Vera responded. "And, yes, I'm turning sixteen tomorrow."

"And I assume that our school's most beloved member of the student body has some grand plans for the special night?"

"I think 'most beloved' is taking it a bit…"

"Actually," Atticus interjected, "I've planned a special birthday present for Vera. She's really into tradition so I figured we would celebrate her birthday the same way we've done for all the years I've known her. Maybe she'll celebrate with everyone another night, but for now I want Ver to remember her sixteenth birthday as a birthday where she got to do what she wanted to do. It is *her* birthday after all. It seems to me that it only makes sense for Vera to choose how to celebrate, whether the student body wants a party or not."

Vera looked up at Atticus with more gratitude and thanks than she imagined she ever could have collected.

"How very gentlemanly of you, Mr. Wells. Then again, I would expect nothing less. As a leader and an educator, I feel that you have truly grown into a fine young man under the tutelage of this institution. Intelligent, and a star athlete to boot! It's young men like you that we are proud to call graduates of Arcadia High School. You're like…specimens that we can point out and call our own."

"With all due respect, Principal McCormac, I don't think specimen is the appropriate word…perhaps role model? Specimen makes Atticus sound like a science experiment. And also, I think he would have done so, become a role model I mean, on his own even without the help of this school. Finch has always been a gentleman." After the words left her, Vera was surprised at her own audacity. Atticus was simply beaming.

"I suppose you're right, Miss Walker. Mr. Wells is, indeed, a gentleman. Now, if you'll excuse me, I need to get back to my writing, and you two should get along to class."

"Have a good day, sir." And with those words, she grabbed Atticus's hand and led him into their English class.

CHAPTER TWO

"How nice it is of you to join us, Miss Walker. And you too, Mr. Wells. It's always a pleasure when the two of you grace us with your collective presence," Miss Barnes, Arcadia High School's honors English teacher, said with a tone that suggested a combination of annoyance and strange understanding. Atticus and Vera had been practically inseparable since the day they met. Separate, they were like any other teenagers; together, they had a presence that no one could quite define.

The entire class turned their heads as Vera and Atticus entered Miss Barnes's English class. Sensing that Miss Barnes was looking for a reason for their tardiness, Vera asserted, without the slightest delay and before being asked, "Finch…I mean Atticus and I were talking to Principal McCormac, Miss Barnes. We're very sorry to have kept you waiting. We just didn't want to leave rudely before he was done speaking."

As usual, Miss Barnes, impressed by the girl's odd talent for knowing what people wanted of her, nodded at the two friends and replied, in her saccharine tone, "Thank you for the explanation. Please take your seats...the both of you. Quickly now."

Miss Barnes was a middle-aged woman with long blonde hair. She wore entirely too much makeup and her exceptionally large body was often adorned with vibrant colors that she liked to call things like "bubblegum pink" and "sunshine yellow." She had quite a shine for Principal McCormac (as far as any of her students could tell) and she had an annoying almost childish way of doing absolutely everything that she could for him. It was as if she hung on to his every word with the hopes that he would one day confess his "undying love for her." Vera often told Atticus that if she ever got the way Miss Barnes does over Principal McCormac around a guy she was seeing, to kindly put her out of her misery lest she turn into an inconsolable, blubbering ball of mush. Atticus never responded to this request, mainly because he never liked picturing Vera falling for any guy but himself. Much to Atticus's dismay, he couldn't bring himself to tell anyone this...*especially* Vera.

Miss Barnes was a genius when it came to literature, which was one of the reasons that Vera was able to tolerate her quirks. However, she lacked, according to Atticus, "any and all social skills." Atticus often joked and said that she reminded him of a rather round fairy princess.

"Class! Now that we're all here and accounted for I have some exciting news for you. I'm proud to announce that this week—"

"Principal McCormac is visiting again and you're going to gawk at him like you usually do?"

Charles Jenkins had always been one to make stupid comments and interrupt teachers. He was the tall, blonde, and chiseled captain and quarterback of the football team and the school's resident "clown" so to speak. His only weakness was Vera, who could always stifle his hurtful comments toward their consistently overwhelmed English teacher. That was possibly the only thing Charles and Vera had in common…they shared a common weakness. Of course Vera's weakness was Atticus, not Charles, though she'd never admit such a weakness to her best friend as she greatly feared any and all potential negative consequences.

"Cut it out, Charles," chimed Vera with a glare in Charles's direction.

Charles's face turned bright red as he muttered, "Sorry, Ver. I was just playing around."

Without a moment's hesitation, Vera continued, "Now what were you going to tell us, Miss Barnes?"

Still flustered but gaining back some of her courage, Miss Barnes decided to try again. "This week our class will be reading one of my favorite novels of all time: *To Kill a Mockingbird* by Harper Lee."

Sitting sullenly at the front of the room, Atticus gave Vera a dismal look and prayed silently to himself that Miss Barnes would gloss over the fact that a boy named Atticus was sitting right in front of her. Atticus cursed the day his parents decided to take the term "literary enthusiasts" to a whole new level. Sure, they had always treasured the written word, but to take that love to the level of naming their son after such a noted fictional character was just too much. It was equivalent to naming a child Ebenezer Scrooge or Harry Potter.

"Furthermore," Miss Barnes continued, "We all should be even more thrilled that one of our own, a student in this very class, shares the first name of the book's unforgettable protagonist. Atticus Wells, you should be so proud to bear such a name."

"Vera," Atticus whispered, a look of pure horror on his face.

"Yeah, Atticus?" Vera said stifling laughter that she knew she couldn't hold in for much longer.

"Shoot me and put me out of my misery. No name is worth this much attention."

"Oh calm down, Finch," Vera said while trying to hold back laughter. "It's really not that bad you know. What's the worst that could happen?"

"Oh I don't know, Ver. She could make me act out a part, read all his lines, dress up all "lawyer-like" like him one day. Or worse she could start using the nickname that *you* find so endearing. The terrible possibilities are endless, my friend. *Endless.*"

"You, my friend, are being a baby. And I honestly don't see the problem with calling you…"

Just as Atticus was about to respond, a high pitched throat was intentionally cleared above them, and Miss Barnes spoke. "Is there something you and Miss Walker would like to share with the rest of the class, Mr. Wells? Or can I continue with my lesson?"

"No…nothing at all. Please continue, Miss Barnes. Sorry," said Atticus while simultaneously giving Vera a dirty look.

"Before we go on with the lesson," Miss Barnes once again continued, "I have one more announcement to make. As you all know, all the teachers at this glorious institution have a class list with names, nicknames, and birthdays…"

"Oh God," Vera whispered.

"This morning, my computer brought to my attention a very special person's birthday. A person who I know all of us hold in very high regard."

"No way… Atticus, this can't be happening…why do they even *have* that list? Is that legal?"

"It is only fitting that we all get a chance to celebrate Miss Vera Walker's sixteenth birthday tomorrow! Remember to have your cupcakes! Fun-fetti!"

And with that announcement, every head in the room turned towards Vera. Sinking slowly down into her chair and leaning toward Atticus, Vera muttered frantically to her best friend, "How exactly do you propose avoiding a huge party *now*, Finch?"

"I think our classmates may have one minor flaw in their plan to celebrate your birthday," Atticus said with a smile.

"And what's that, Atticus?"

"Do you trust me?"

"Come on, Finch, of course I trust you. Just *tell me!*"

"Leave it to me, Ver. No one will be around to bug you tomorrow."

And with those words Vera sank easily into her chair and smiled widely at Atticus.

CHAPTER THREE

Vera was bombarded by a sea of people after class.

"Why didn't you tell us it was your birthday, Vera?"

"When's the big party?"

"Am I invited?"

"When did you make the invitation list?"

"Did my invite to your Sweet Sixteen get lost in the mail?"

"How am I supposed to get you a present with so little time, Ver?" Charles asked, "I thought we were tight? You know, I thought you were one of my girls."

"If by tight, Charles, you mean that you stare at her butt as she walks down the hall and frequently tell her that she has a 'smokin' hot bod' then yeah... I guess you're tight. Not exactly my definition of tight, but to each his own," Vera's friend from art class, Ashliana Johnson, a tiny blonde girl with chocolate brown eyes that seemed to emanate kindness, stated, giving Vera a small smile and a wink. Ash's boyfriend, Evan Alton, Atticus's best friend from the soccer team, stood next to her and stared down Charles as if to repeat what she said without saying a single word. Evan had the same build as Atticus, but with blonde hair and brown eyes similar to Ashliana's- just his presence in a room astronomically brightened its atmosphere. Both Evan and Ashliana were aware of the reasoning behind Vera's aversion to her own birthday, and thus always made sticking up for their friend a priority.

Sensing that he was losing power in the situation, Charles quickly decided to use his most utilized defense mechanism: his insults and cruel words. "Sarcasm not appreciated, Ash. You and I both know that Vera here is beautiful... and don't try to say you're not, Miss Vera. But, my sweet Ver, we both also know that you're a tease. A tease who's afraid of commitment," he remarked in his most pompous tone. "You would be lucky to have a guy like me. Just face it, Ver, you're arm candy and that's all everyone in this school sees you as. So you should just swallow your pride and let me take you to dinner sometime."

Atticus didn't know whether it was the "arm candy" or the "swallow your pride" part of Charles's harangue that made his insides want to explode, but before Evan could even attempt to stop him, or anyone else could blink an eye, Atticus's fist had collided with Charles's jaw. Charles's head swung to the side as he fell almost immediately to the floor, cursing as soon as he could speak.

"Smooth, dude," Evan said laughing at his enraged friend, "Real controlled. Good thing Principal McCormac likes you."

Trying to hold in the rest of his anger, Atticus spoke slowly and deliberately to Charles, now lying on the floor in front of him, his lip bleeding slightly from Atticus's strong punch.

"Never, EVER, speak to Vera like that again, you hear me? I may not be a bully or a tough guy, but one thing I will not stand for is dim-witted losers putting my friends down...*any* of my friends, and especially Vera. And for the record," Atticus said, finally calming down, "If you like a girl...insulting her may not be the best way to win her affections. *Just saying.*"

"Well put, Atticus," Ashliana said before looking at Charles and, with a grin, saying, "Yep...you and Ver...you're the *epitome of tight*. Come on, Ev, it's time for track practice."

And with that, Atticus put his hand on Vera's shoulder and led her away from Charles and the crowd that had accrued. Vera, dumbstruck, was at a loss for words as her best friend led her to the school's exit as the end of the day school bell rang.

CHAPTER FOUR

Vera and Atticus walked down the sidewalk towards Atticus's house. Vera could tell that he was still upset over what had happened in the school as he was walking abnormally fast and had his "I want to punch a wall" expression on his face. He also wasn't saying a word which, in Vera's experience, meant he was either angry, deep in thought, or possibly both.

Looking at Atticus, a passerby might get the impression that he was the stereotypical "popular jock guy," but he was far from that person. Atticus was, in Vera's opinion, incredibly good looking in a sweet and geeky sort of way, but he was also unbelievably modest. He always had others' best interests at heart and he had a habit of remaining calm in any situation, which was why Vera was so startled when Atticus punched Charles. Even in elementary school Atticus used to walk away from fights (fights Vera knew he would have won)…and even Vera got in a few fights in elementary school. Atticus was one of those people who was protective, but exceedingly kind…he only used violence as a last resort.

Vera also worried because Atticus's eyes, the one part of him that always made Vera feel safe and secure, looked way too serious. Vera loved Atticus's eyes because, in her opinion, they were both his strong point and his weak point: they showed not only his benevolence, humanity, honesty, and his ability to protect, but also his vulnerabilities. His eyes made him an "open book"; he could rarely hide his emotions from anyone. Atticus hated that about himself, but Vera loved him for it.

In an attempt to make Atticus feel better, Vera finally spoke. "Thanks for defending me like that, Finch. It was really good of you, and you know you didn't have to help me. Charles is an idiot, he always has been...he doesn't bother me...you know that, right? *Atticus*?"

"He had no right to talk to you like that, Ver. What he said was rude and completely untrue. I know I didn't have to defend you. I wanted to defend you, Vera. You're my friend and you mean the world to me. You shouldn't have to deal with being treated like you're less than who you are. No one deserves to be treated like that."

Vera blushed and put her eyes down to the ground. She often wondered how she was lucky enough to be Atticus Wells's best friend. He never failed to surprise her with his capacity for kindness and his unfailing loyalty. In all the years she had known him, from their first day at pre-school together up until that very moment, Vera never witnessed Atticus's unwavering faithfulness falter. He was the best person Vera knew.

Simply put, even though Atticus had grown into a fine young adult, to Vera he was still the kind-hearted little boy who had invited her, the new girl with absolutely no friends and a shy way about her, to sit next to him on their first day of pre-school even though all the boys pointed and laughed and sang love songs in his face. Atticus had stared them down and then continued talking to Vera without even flinching. Without Atticus, Vera wouldn't have become as good or strong or confident a person. Vera needed Atticus more than anyone else in the world.

"You mean the world to me too, Finch," Vera replied wishing she could express her feelings in a better way than just those few words. Just as she was attempting to think of something better to say, Vera realized she and Atticus were just a mere few steps from Atticus's house.

Vera loved going to Atticus's house because it always felt like a "home" to her. When she was growing up she spent more time at Atticus's house than at her own house. This was mainly because her adoptive parents were blessed with twins when she was five years old and slowly but surely seemed to have less and less time for their oldest adopted daughter. Vera's parents were still kind to her, but the understanding, independent, and intelligent little girl knew that she didn't fit, and would probably never fit.

Vera *belonged* at Atticus's house. She spent most of her weekday afternoons there as a child and often spent the night on weekends. The Wells house was a place that represented safety, warmth, and happiness for Vera, and Mr. and Mrs. Wells saw her as their daughter. Tonight was meant to be "Vera's Birthday" at the Wellses' house; Mr. and Mrs. Wells knew that they couldn't keep Vera on her actual birthday so they insisted on having her over the night before.

"I can't believe your parents are throwing me a party, Atticus."

"I can. My parents think you're God's gift to the world. They love you like a daughter, I'm pretty sure they like you more than me, and I know they would feel like they missed out on something if they didn't celebrate your birthday." And with those words Atticus opened his front door and led Vera into the house.

CHAPTER FIVE

"Vera!" Mr. and Mrs. Wells were practically flinging themselves on Vera as she walked through the door.

"Mom…Dad…don't crush her to death," Atticus said midlaugh, "It's not like you don't see her every day! Besides, I like having a *living* best friend, thank you very much!"

"Oh, let us be sentimental, Atticus Jeremy. You know Vera is like a daughter to us," Mrs. Wells interjected. "Plus, it's nice having another girl in the house…I'm always so outnumbered with Atticus and Dean."

"Really, Mom? The middle name?" Atticus asked rolling his eyes.

"Yes really, *Atticus Jeremy Wells*," Vera said stretching upward to put her arm around his shoulder and then turning her face upwards towards his with a sarcastic but at the same time lovely smile, "And, Mr. and Mrs. Wells, it's always nice to be here." Vera looked around at the familiar, safe haven that was the Wells house. Vera loved every part of the house from the living room that doubled as a library (complete with every genre of literature in existence from horror to children's books), to the basement area which served as

Vera and Atticus's "hang out" that included a foosball table, pool table, and an air hockey table. Atticus's house was unbelievable.

The only televisions in the Wells house were in the basement and in Atticus's bedroom as Atticus was the only Wells who used them. Mr. and Mrs. Wells always asserted that they were content reading their newspapers, though they did indulge in television for important global, national, or political events. After admiring the house for the millionth time, Vera suddenly became aware of a few changes.

"The two of you really shouldn't have done all this for me." Vera wasn't being modest while making this statement. The Wellses had blown up balloons, hung up streamers, baked a home-made cake (chocolate of course without frosting, Vera's favorite), and, by the looks of it, had gone out and bought Vera a few gifts as well.

"You know it's always our pleasure to do this for you, Vera. You keep Atticus in line for me."

"Mr. Wells, Atticus hardly needs watching. He looks after me more than I do him. Seriously, he's like Kevin Costner in *The Bodyguard*."

"First of all, Ver, I'd like to think of myself more as Kevin Costner from *Robin Hood: Prince of Thieves*, because you're more like Maid Marion…you know for a noble woman she was brave and could really take care of herself, and when she decided to deliver that letter to King Richard and got captured…"

Mr. and Mrs. Wells stood still looking back and forth between Vera and Atticus. Both the Wells parents knew that once the two friends started in on one of these arguments, any outside observer simply had to wait for the culmination patiently. Vera versus Atticus arguments were not ones that were entered or stopped lightly.

"Atticus, I was just giving your parents an example, but if you want to get picky about it then…"

"And the whole I look after you more thing? Not true, Ver. Just the other day you explained that really difficult poem to me, you know that one by Robert Frost...the 'Two roads diverged in a yellow wood, and sorry I could not travel both' one."

"Atticus, that is *not* a difficult poem," Vera said with a tone of indignation, "It is a simple extended metaphor with a universal message...one that is especially powerful as it can apply to any and every individual, and I think you understood it perfectly well before you asked me. And furthermore..."

"Oh, Ver, don't say 'furthermore,' it makes you sound pretentious."

"It does not make me sound pretentious! Just because *I* read, Atticus..."

"I read!" Atticus said his face contorted with an affronted look. "Obviously not *Robert Frost.*"

"Well...*fine*, okay, maybe I forgot to read *that* poem. But, hey, that still proves my point! I would've looked like a complete idiot in front of Miss Barnes if it weren't for *you*. And why are we even arguing about 'who takes care of who' more anyway, *Vera Eleanor*? It's idiotic."

"It's *not* idiotic, *Atticus Jeremy* and, yes, you would have looked like an illiterate idiot..."

"Illiterate is taking it a bit too far, don't you—"

"*But* that still doesn't prove your point. Take today, for instance...Atticus, just today, you *punched someone* for me."

"Vera!" Atticus hissed at her, but too late to stop the words from entering his parents' ears, "A little tact from the walking dictionary would be nice."

"I am NOT a walking..." but she was promptly interrupted by Mrs. Wells's booming, angry voice.

"Atticus Jeremy Wells," Mrs. Wells scolded rounding on her son until she was face to face with him, "You punched someone today?"

Vera fidgeted uncomfortably and gave Atticus the best "I'm sorry" look she could muster. After a few seconds of silence and evil looks from Mrs. Wells in Atticus's direction, Vera decided to explain the situation.

"Atticus was defending me, Mr. and Mrs. Wells. This boy in our class, Charles Jenkins, you probably know him, he's popular but not really the good sort."

"Vera. You don't need to explain..." but Vera continued her speech, evidently oblivious to Atticus's previous statement.

"Anyways... he said some really hurtful things to me this afternoon. I usually put up a good front so that people will believe that I'm not upset. I'm actually really good at it, and everyone falls for it... well, everyone except your son, and sometimes Ash and Ev, but mostly just your son. He saw that I was hurt and he stuck up for me...in the form of punching Charles in the face. To be frank..."

"I'd rather you'd just be Vera..." Atticus said trying to lighten the mood of the room to no avail.

"Atticus," Vera said with great exasperation, "If you want me to explain then don't make fun of my use of the English language," and then turning back to Mr. and Mrs. Wells she, again, continued, "As I was saying, *to be frank*, I don't think words would have gotten through to Charles," Vera said without much thought. And upon seeing Atticus's parents' faces change from understanding to disappointment once again, Vera back-peddled, talking rapidly, "Not that I'm an advocate of violence, but I mean, in this particular case...if you were there...what I'm saying is...please don't be angry with Atticus. I could have stopped him and I only said something to let you know how much I appreciate him protecting me...and, of course, to prove my point, but that's really besides the point... *this point* not that 'I was right about the argument' point. What I'm trying to tell you is, if you're going to punish him or ground him you should call my parents and..."

"We're not going to ground Atticus, Vera," said Mr. Wells, kindly holding back laughter.

"You're not?" Vera asked looking back and forth between the Wells parents, "Oh…then we're cool?"

"Almost. Good speech, Vera," Mr. Wells said with a slightly comical nod.

"Oh…well thank you. But if it was a good explanation, then why are we only almost cool instead of…" but Vera was interrupted by Mr. Wells who now faced Atticus and spoke.

"Atticus…did you get a good swing at this boy?"

"Yeah, I think so, Dad. He fell to the floor pretty hard…I think his lip may have been bleeding too. I wasn't really paying attention to be honest."

"I am witness to the fact that there was, in fact, blood," Vera declared excitedly and factually.

"Good, because if any son of mine tried to punch a kid and did it wrong then that would be just shameful."

"No worries, Mr. Wells. Atticus carries some heavy ammunition."

With that, all four of them began to laugh, as Vera was never one to make reference to anything having to do with "ammunition." By the end of the night, Vera and Atticus would have completely forgotten who won the "who takes more care of who" argument.

CHAPTER SIX

Atticus made his way up the steps toward the Walker Family front porch. He could think of no better day to celebrate Vera's sixteenth birthday; the sun was shining, and it was unusually warm for a spring day in the tiny town of Seckerlyn Center in northern Vermont. Atticus also felt a strange sense of pride that he was the one celebrating Vera's birthday with her…though why he was proud or beyond happy he didn't know. Just the day before Vera seemed to express no interest in partying with the so called "popular" kids in the school, but on the phone that morning Vera had seemed thrilled to spend the day with him.

Even though he was aware of Vera's excitement about her birthday, Atticus still approached the house with hesitation. He honestly cared for Vera more than he cared for anyone, and if he messed up anything about her birthday he knew he would never forgive himself. Today had to be incredible…just like his best friend who, despite the fact that she amazed him one moment and annoyed the life out of him the next, he desperately wanted to become something more…

Slowly but surely Atticus finally made it to the door and rang the doorbell. After only a few seconds, Vera opened the door. She was wearing a simple yet formal looking midnight blue top and a mid-length brown skirt with pleats. The shirt's color made Vera's eyes pop, causing her to seem even more intimidating to Atticus than usual. But the one thing that Atticus noticed most of all, was that Vera was beaming; she looked unbelievably happy.

Vera looked back up at Atticus with incredible admiration. She was pleased that he had chosen his maroon sweater and dark jeans as she thought they always made him look even more attractive than he did on a daily basis. She initially noticed his nervousness, which seemed odd to Vera because she felt as if she was the one that should act nervous around Atticus. *Atticus* had hordes of girls tailing him at school. *Atticus* looked comfortable in any situation. *Atticus* could win an entire crowd of people over just by smiling at them. *Atticus* already had college coaches recruiting him for soccer. *Atticus* seemed to be completely oblivious to his own popularity.

But for some reason, Atticus looked on edge. This nervousness, however, didn't last very long. Almost seconds after perceiving Atticus's anxiety, Vera could have sworn that it was never there in the first place, because he was looking down at her with the biggest smile she'd seen in a long, long time. Something in the way he smiled at her made Vera feel wanted, protected, and loved. Atticus always had a way about him that made Vera implausibly happy.

"You ready for your big day, Ver?" Atticus asked in a semi-scripted yet humorous tone.

"You're ridiculous, Finch. You know you didn't have to plan an epic day-long birthday celebration for me. I would have been happy with the traditional Vera Walker boring birthday."

"Your birthdays were never boring, Ver. I just thought we'd shake things up a little bit, even though I told Principal McCormac I wouldn't."

"But, Atticus, it's Saturday…and you're going to the shops in Burlington…with *just me*."

Noting the opening for some type of sarcasm, Atticus replied, "Well, 'just you,' what else am I supposed to do on a Saturday?"

"Oh, I don't know, Atticus. Maybe go to Melyssa Marshall's annual 'Spring Fling Bash' with all the other cool kids? She has a thing for you, you know…Melyssa Marshall…has since the second grade I think. *Definitely* since then because I remember her giving you way too many Valentines that year…it was creepy, Finch. Though, you seemed…*flattered.* Plus she's captain of the cheerleading squad…there's an automatic popularity boost for you. Going once…going twice…"

"Yeah, *okay.* It's not just us boycotting that fiasco of a party… Ev and Ash aren't going either. Besides I'll date Melyssa when you date Charles, Vera Walker."

Vera, a little taken aback, attempted to put the ball back in her friend's metaphorical court. "Who said anything about dating, Finch? I didn't mention dating. I merely reminded you of her party. You brought up dating… is there something you're not telling me? Do you have all those Valentines stashed in a secret spot somewhere? Do you have a secret floorboard where you keep them all? Oooo, show me!"

"Come on, Ver. You know I would rather go to your precious debutante ball five times over than spend one second at Melyssa Marshall's Spring Fling Bash. Especially considering the undeniable fact that Charles will be there…probably staring at you the entire night…and by you, I mean your butt. That in itself would drive me completely over the edge. No one is mean, or inappropriate, to my girl."

"First of all, the debutante ball…was not my idea. That was ALL my mom and you know that! You know I didn't want to wear that stupid dress and parade around like I was the most important person on the face of the planet. My mom was on a rampage about how I didn't want to be a debutante and how everyone in her family was and how I was letting them down, and I just couldn't take it anymore, Finch! And secondly," and at this point Vera paused in order to formulate the appropriate wording in her head, "I'm *your girl* now?"

Atticus turned bright red. Hoping to rectify the situation and negate any awkwardness, he hesitantly said, "Well, you know what I mean. Like 'you ma girl'," he said in his most gangster sounding voice.

"So, I'm your girl in the gangster rap sense?" Vera asked, secretly hoping this wasn't the case.

"Yes... I mean no... I mean—"

"I thought you two would be out and about by now," interrupted Mrs. Walker.

"We were just about to head out, Mom. Where's Dad?"

"Since Atticus has you for the day he figured he could get in an extra day at the office and get back in time for cake tonight."

Vera's dad was a lawyer— a very good lawyer. He practiced criminal law and was the reason Vera was obsessed with solving problems and mysteries and such. She was also great at debating. No one could come close to out-talking her once she got going... she was like the Energizer Bunny of big, powerful words. She just kept going and going and going. No one, that is, except for Atticus who had, over the years, gotten strangely used to her brilliant use of sarcasm and wit and had subsequently come up with his own devious ways to combat her in heated discussions.

"Where are the boys, Mrs. Walker?" Atticus asked politely.

Vera's twin brothers loved Atticus. They thought he was the coolest person in the entire world because he played imaginary games with them. Atticus was the best sword fighter and the best hide and seeker and the best person to use for a pony ride, according to the loud, athletic prankster Sebastian. His twin Benedict, the more practical, logical, and serious of the two, enjoyed Atticus because he read to him.

"Oh they're around, Atticus. I'm surprised they didn't come running out at the sound of your voice."

"Maybe they didn't hear me," Atticus said in a booming voice.

Not a second later, loud footsteps were heard on the stairs inside the Walker house.

"Finch!" An excited Sebastian arrived in the doorway first and jumped up into Atticus's arms. "Come and play sword fight with us!"

"Sorry, Bastian. I can't sword fight today. I'm…"

"Or we could read or tell stories," interrupted Benedict who showed up seconds after his brother, "I know you like that better, Finch."

"It's not that I don't like the game, Ben… it's just, today I'm taking your sister out for her birthday. Maybe I can play sword fight and read later."

"Are you dating my sister?" the ever curious and intelligent Benedict asked.

"Yeah, are you?" echoed his twin in an annoying, questioning tone.

Atticus, looking a little down-trodden answered, "Right now, Ver and I are just friends."

Sensing his awkwardness, Vera piped in. "Yeah, you both know Atticus and I have been best friends since like… well since we met." She smiled at Atticus hoping these words eased his discomfort.

However, before Atticus could respond, the boys jumped in again. "Yeah, we know that, Ver. But everyone knows that you and Atticus are gonna get married," Benedict said, completely serious.

"We're ten, Ver. We're not dumb… we see right through both of you," chimed in Sebastian.

"Alright, boys, that's enough. Yes, it *would* be wonderful if Atticus and Vera got married someday…"

"Mom!" Vera said flabbergasted, her eyes fluttering nervously, but Mrs. Walker continued anyway.

"…Because we all love Atticus. Right now I think we should just let them go have a good time for Vera's birthday."

"On that note, we're gonna get going. Love you, Mom! See you later, boys!"

And as quickly as she could, Vera grabbed Atticus's hand tightly and pulled him away from the house and towards the bus stop-away from what had become a sea of awkwardness.

CHAPTER SEVEN

Vera and Atticus hopped off the bus as quickly as possible upon arriving in Downtown Burlington. There were several stops on Atticus's list to ensure Vera had the best birthday imaginable: Uncommon Grounds (their favorite coffee shop) to wake them up, Bove's of Vermont for an Italian Dinner, Ben & Jerry's Ice Cream for dessert, and of course all the book, movie, and music stores in the area. Atticus had been planning this day for a long time and wasn't going to let anything mess it up.

Atticus had called ahead to Ben & Jerry's so that Vera could have a "Vermonster" sundae delivered right to their table at exactly 7:14pm: the precise time Vera was born. Therefore, Atticus knew the two had to stay on their eating and shopping schedule in order to arrive at Ben & Jerry's at around 7:00pm. Atticus considered the amount of work that he had put into the planning of Vera's birthday…and for a second found himself asking if he was nuts to care this much. After all, it *was* just a birthday…but at the same time, it *wasn't*. It was a celebration for Vera…and Vera was more than just a best friend to Atticus…she was a kindred spirit, and the only person in the world who knew him for exactly who he was.

"So, how does Uncommon Grounds sound? Possibly followed by a Barnes & Noble visit funded by yours truly?"

Vera did an unintentional excited jump and replied, "Really, Finch? You're going to pay for my books?"

"The whole day is on me, Ver…coffee, dinner, ice cream, and your choice of five books, if you want that many, from Barnes & Noble."

"Five?!?! Oh my gosh, thank you! I just finished the book I got last weekend and I was hoping to find time to get another book soon…you know I blow through books like it's my job. But five, Atticus? Are you sure? "

"It's your birthday, Ver. It should be special."

"How am I going to match this for your birthday? I don't think I could if I tried…unless we went to some epic amusement park or something…I'm gonna have to get tickets now…ohhhh, we could go to Six Flags!!!"

"Let's worry about that when it comes, Vera. Just enjoy today, okay?"

"Sounds good to me, Finch. And I know I'm probably going to be saying this all day, but thank you for this. Already, this is the best birthday I've ever had…nobody has ever planned this many amazing things just for me. I feel like I don't quite deserve all of this"

Atticus gave Vera a confused look. How could she not think she deserved a day just for her? She was always thinking about other people…she needed a day dedicated to herself. The girl honestly never thought of what was best for her; it was always "What would be best for Ben and Bastian?" "What would make Mom and Dad happy?" "What would be fun to do with Ev and Ash?" "How to help around home and school." Vera put others before herself as a rule, and her friend knew she needed a break. Finally Atticus spoke, "You deserve this, Vera. Trust me."

And smiling, Atticus took Vera's hand and led her into Uncommon Grounds.

⟫⟪

With bags in hand full of books, CDs, DVDs, and Bove's leftovers, Vera and Atticus walked into Ben & Jerry's. It was 7:10pm... just enough time for them to get a table before Vera's surprise "Vermonster" was due to arrive. Vera and Atticus sat down at a small table right in the middle of the room: the only one left as it was unbelievably crowded in the ice cream parlor.

Atticus waited until Vera sat down and then went over to the counter to tell the workers that they were ready for the ice cream. The ice cream was brought out a tad early, so Atticus decided that a countdown was in order.

"One minute until the great Vera Walker's birthday!" Atticus said excitedly.

"Please, Atticus, there's definitely no need for a countdown. It's my birthday not New Year's Eve."

"Come on, Ver. Live a little...45, 44, 43..."

"Atticus, stop, it's embarrassing," Vera said half shyly half with vigor.

"30, 29, 28, 27..." Atticus continued – a hint of laughter in his voice.

"Seriously Finch, my sixteenth birthday isn't this big of a deal. Really, it might as well be a normal day. A school day. A *Monday*."

"10, 9, 8, 7..."

"Oh, whatever...4, 3, 2, 1..."

Atticus's "Happy Birthday" was drowned out by what seemed to Vera as a million voices talking to her all at once. Instinctively, Vera put her hands up to her ears.

Wow, that girl's hot...
> *Do these jeans make my butt look big?...*
>> *What if he doesn't like me?...*
Man, I could go for a burrito...
> *Shoot, I'm late...*
>> *Forgot to feed the dog...*
Gotta pick up the kids from swimming...
> *Maybe I should have gotten the blue bikini...*
>> *It's beautiful outside...*
I really don't want to write my bio paper...
> *Why are girls so difficult?...*
>> *So if I study chem now...I can study Brit Lit later...*
He's with her! Oh my God, I'm going to vomit...
> *If my brother pokes me...one more time...*

Vera couldn't seem to turn it off. Every person she looked at, she heard. But none of their mouths were moving. In a panic, Vera looked at Atticus and spoke rapidly and haphazardly, "I have to go...I'm...I'm sorry, Finch."

"Vera, wait," Atticus called after her, but to no avail. He watched as she sprinted down the street without even a glance back at him. For the first time in his life, Atticus felt the bitter sting of inferiority. What had he done? Why wouldn't she even grace him with an answer as she ran down the street?

Vera ran out of Ben & Jerry's toward the bus stop...

What does she think she's doing?
> *Oooo, I like that necklace...*
>> *Did I turn off the lights?*
I hate my life...
> *Oooo, a dollar!*
>> *I wish I had the money to buy that dress...*

Vera kept running, cupping her hands over her ears hoping the voices would go away. Within a minute, tears began to stream down her face, and she knew she had to find a way to hide them... she hated crying in public. She hated crying *period*. But every person she looked at seemed to scream at her relentlessly.

Vera stopped at the closest sun-glasses stand, bought the first pair she saw, and shoved them on her face. Suddenly, everything went silent. Vera looked around at everyone who passed, but this time she couldn't hear anything.

Out of curiosity, Vera carefully took off the glasses; instantly the voices came back...

> *I hope it doesn't rain.*
> *I want to go camping!*
> *My brother gets everything!*

Quickly, Vera slipped the glasses back on. Again the voices were silenced. Vera walked slowly but deliberately back to the glasses stand and picked out the most normal looking pair of fake non-prescription clear glasses and switched them out with the sunglasses. Then, still crying, Vera walked to the bus station, got on the bus, rode home without talking to or looking at anyone, told her parents she was sick and not to worry about the cake, laid down on her bed, and cried until she fell asleep, thinking all the while about how she knew for sure that she had destroyed whatever relationship she could have had with Atticus.

CHAPTER EIGHT

Vera walked onto Atticus's front porch and rang the doorbell. She couldn't believe what was happening to her, and if *she* couldn't believe it, then how in the world was Atticus going to believe her? She didn't even know if she could tell Atticus what she came over his house to say. While these thoughts continued to race through her head, the door swung open.

In the doorway stood Atticus; his face looked sad and frustrated as he spoke to her. "Come to explain why you ditched me yesterday? Why after I planned an awesome birthday for you, one that I knew you would love, you randomly left just when we were going to have dessert, said that you just had to leave, that you were 'sorry', and then ran away before I could even utter a word?"

"Atticus, will you please let me in so I can explain myself?"

"I called after you! You didn't even turn around! I went after you!"

"Atticus, please let me talk!"

"Why should I?"

"Please...don't you trust me?" Vera asked in desperation.

Atticus looked at Vera. What she had done had confused him, but the look in her eyes told him that he should trust her, give her a chance to explain herself. His expression toward her changed to one of trust and understanding as he opened the door and let Vera inside. As she passed, Atticus noticed another change in Vera that his anger before had prevented him from observing: since when did she wear glasses?

Vera sat down on Atticus's living room couch. She felt so at home in Atticus's house; just being there gave Vera more courage. While contemplating just how she was going to tell Atticus, she suddenly became aware that he was staring at her.

"Atticus, please stop staring at me."

"I'm not staring at you, Ver; I'm staring at your glasses. Since when do you need glasses? I've known you forever and you've always bragged about your perfect vision."

Taken aback, Vera quickly replied, "I do not brag!"

Rolling his eyes, Atticus continued, "Oh, you know what I mean. Can't you at least tell me why you're wearing them? You know you can trust me."

"I just like them, okay?"

"You just like them? You, Vera Walker, are a terrible liar. Always have been...always will be."

Atticus needn't have told Vera that. Vera had never been a good liar, especially when it came to lying to Atticus. It was close to impossible for her to lie to him since she cared about him so much...not to mention the fact that she considered lying to the person she trusted the most to be shameful...

"I'm not lying, Atticus! I think they make me look...well...smart."

With a smirk and a slight jilt of laughter Atticus responded, "I hate to break it to you, Ver, but you don't need glasses to look smart. Come to think of it, you're probably on the bottom of the 'people who need to change their appearances' list." At this, Vera unknowingly began to blush.

"Even though you are probably one of the biggest nerds I know..."

"One of the biggest nerds you know? Seriously, Finch..."

"Every guy in this school has wanted to date you since they figured out the joys and mysteries of the dating world," Atticus finished interrupting her defense.

"I'm not interested in dating them, Finch. They don't know me...they only like me because I'm reasonably attractive and..."

At these words, Atticus did a double take. Did she actually call herself reasonably attractive? Maybe she really did need glasses...

"Hold on, Ver. First of all, I have told you over and over again not to call me Finch. Having a first name like 'Atticus' is bad enough. Having you call me Finch is taking it an entirely new level of geek."

"Atticus, for the millionth time, although you don't like your literary name, you should be proud to be named for such a dynamic protagonist in one of my favorite books. *To Kill a Mockingbird* is a classic novel that was way ahead of its time and influenced several generations of readers and..."

Atticus quickly interrupted her...he'd heard this diatribe before, "And second of all, did you really just call yourself 'reasonably attractive'?"

"Yes...why? Was that too snobby?"

"Too snobby?!?! Vera Walker, you are, by far, the most beautiful girl in our school." And with those words, Atticus averted Vera's glace and looked down at the floor. He couldn't face her eyes after saying what he said. Those eyes already could read him too well.

"I didn't know you thought that about me." Vera asked shyly.

Finally looking up at her again, realizing that she wasn't repulsed by the idea of him thinking she was beautiful, Atticus found his friend's eyes and said, "Always have, Ver, and that's why, among other reasons, you know you can trust me. Just tell me why you're wearing those glasses…tell me what's going on! I just want to know the truth. And, well, if you're not going to explain yourself, you should just leave because I deserve an explanation. Please, Ver. Trust me."

Vera looked at Atticus's face, and into his eyes. Atticus was the person Vera trusted the most in the world. He was her best friend, and the person who knew her better than anyone else. But how could she tell him this? What if he didn't believe her? Or what if he did, and never talked to her again?

She had to know before she told him. With reluctance, Vera slid her glasses down below her eyes and looked at Atticus.

I wish she would just let me in. She knows I would never hurt her, never abandon her…hell, I would die for her. If by now she can't see that, then why have we stayed friends for this long? It just doesn't make sense… why won't she trust me? She means so much to me…I just hope I mean just as much to her…enough at least for her to tell me the truth…

Vera put her glasses back to her eyes…she had heard enough. "Atticus? I have something that I need to tell you. It might sound crazy or freak you out but I need to tell someone and you're the most important person in my world right now so I think you'd be my best choice."

"Go ahead, Ver. I promise I won't judge you or anything."

"It's going to sound crazy."

"Try me."

"*Really* crazy."

"Just tell me, Vera."

Vera took a deep breath. "Okay, so you know how you're always telling me that you feel like I know you too well like I can read your thoughts?"

"Yeah…"

"Well, what if I told you that starting last night on the exact time of my birthday, 7:14pm, I developed the ability to hear *everyone's* thoughts...I can...*I can read minds, Atticus.* I can read minds and I...I don't know how to stop it. It scares me, and I...I..."

And with her last few words, Vera fell into Atticus and began to cry. Atticus, shocked and confused, held her tightly and rubbed her back saying over and over, "I believe you...it's okay."

CHAPTER NINE

"So this started happening at the exact time of your birthday?" Atticus asked once Vera began to calm down.

"Yes. It was like everyone was talking to me at the same time. I couldn't concentrate on anything, Finch. I didn't know how to tell you at that exact moment, because *I* didn't even understand what was going on…I ran to the closest sun-glasses stand to pick up a pair to hide the fact that I was crying hysterically, and that's when I found out that glasses block out the thoughts."

"Who else knows about this, Ver? Did you tell Ash?"

Vera lowered her eyes to the ground as if deep in thought and then replied, "No one knows but you…I haven't even told my parents yet."

"You chose *me* to tell?" Atticus asked with a hint of both surprise and satisfaction, "Why?"

"It's obvious isn't it? You're *Atticus*…you're *my person*. I thought that was kind of obvious, actually."

"*Your person*? Your person for what exactly? Explain please, Ver."

"It's hard to explain," Vera began before turning away in deep thought, "I guess it's something, a concept or a truth that I've believed in forever. During your life you meet all different people. Some stay your friends, some become your enemies, and some you may even grow to love. And in the midst of all of these arrivals and departures, meetings and goodbyes, friendships and rivalries you find someone...someone who understands you wholly. Sometimes you meet this person when you're young, sometimes you meet them when you're old, and, tragically, sometimes you never meet. But I know, indubitably, that each of us has such a person, and this person can look at you and see not just what you are to the world but also who you are to yourself and who you strive to be. And that, Atticus...that's what you are to me."

Vera turned around to face Atticus; her eyes bore into him as if searching for something more than just understanding or affirmation. It was as if her eyes sought truth itself as she waited the few seconds it took for Atticus's response – seconds that, to Vera, seemed like hours.

"In that case...you're my person too, Vera...even though I have to look up every other word you say to me in the dictionary," Atticus said with a sideways grin.

The two locked eyes for a moment before Atticus decided to break the trance they seemed to have fallen into. "Okay," he said while getting up from the couch and beginning to pace around the room. "Maybe you have to look directly at people in order to read their thoughts. As long as there's something between your eyes and the person near you, you're safe from hearing their thoughts. That's why you can't hear anything when your eyes are closed. As long as your wear the glasses, you can keep it in check."

"But I don't want to have to depend on a pair of fake glasses my whole life, Atticus! I want to be able to walk around without worrying about what would happen if the glasses ever went missing or something…without feeling like a complete freak. I need to learn to control this!"

Atticus had never seen his friend so desperate before, and that scared him. Hoping to rectify the situation as much as possible and calm Vera down, Atticus decided to speak. "Maybe you can practice on me. You know, practice controlling the thoughts by reading mine. Take your glasses off…you'll be able to read my thoughts and see if there's anything you can do to stop hearing them. It's worth a try right?"

"I guess so, Finch. But isn't that a huge invasion of your privacy? What if I hear something you don't want me to hear?"

"That's a risk I'll have to take I guess…I'm willing to take that risk to help you."

After a slight pause, Vera sighed and said, "Alright, here it goes," and Vera took her glasses off and looked at Atticus.

Wow, this is really weird…Ver is probably hearing this whole stupid conversation I'm having in my head right now…oooo, I wonder if I can ask a question and get an answer? That would be cool. Okay…hey, Ver, what's your favorite color?

"You know my favorite color, Atticus. But just to appease your thoughts, it's cerulean blue," Vera said half annoyed and half amused.

That is so cool…I'm really hungry…maybe Ver will be up for a cheeseburger run after we do this whole mind-reading experiment.…yeah, we can stop and get burgers and then…wait…oh crap. We can't get burgers, the Spring Fling is tonight. Oh crap…OH CRAP. Why am I always such an idiot…it wasn't Ver's fault she left yesterday. Way to go, Atticus…get mad at your best friend and then do the stupidest thing you can think of to get back at her. Why on earth did I say yes to her? I hate Melyssa Marshall… Vera hates Melyssa Marshall…but stupid Atticus is going to Spring Fling with her…I hate myself…wait… Vera?… Did you just hear all that? Atticus thought…his eyes rising up to meet Vera's.

"I heard it," Vera answered quietly and put her glasses back on, "Were you going to tell me at all, Finch? That you were going to the dance with Melyssa?"

"Vera, I didn't want you to hear it like that...and it sort of just happened really quickly. But you heard what I was thinking...I don't want to go at all. She asked me last night after you had run away and I was really upset. I was sad so I said yes. I only did it to..."

"To get back at me and hurt me like I hurt you? Real mature, Atticus."

"Vera, I didn't want to hurt you...I wanted to make you...never mind."

"Make me what, Atticus? Make me feel inadequate? Make me feel uncomfortable?"

"No! Why would I want to do that to you?"

"Oh, I don't know...maybe because I ditched you in Burlington yesterday and you got mad at me?"

"Vera, I was thrilled that you even wanted to hang out with just me for the day...I put you on a pedestal day in and day out. I was mad at myself for thinking I was good enough to spend the day with you."

"That's so stupid, Atticus. We have been friends for years and you think that I would rather hang out with someone like Charles than with you? You must think very little of me."

"I think the world of you, Vera! How can you even say that?"

"Well, maybe I don't know you as well as I thought. Maybe I was wrong to think that you were different from all the other guys out there. You're just as selfish, stupid, and immature as the other jerks in our school."

"You know what, Vera....forget it. You obviously weren't listening that closely to what I was thinking. Maybe reading people's thoughts makes you judgmental instead of aware. Think whatever you want, Ver. I don't care anymore. There, now I really am just like those other guys."

Atticus's last words hit Vera like a ton of bricks. He didn't care anymore. Hurt and defeated, Vera finally spoke. "I think I'm going to go home. Get into my dress for the dance...I guess I'll see you there?"

"Yeah. I'll see you there," Atticus answered sullenly after an awkward silence.

Vera walked towards the door and turned the handle. Just as she was about to walk out the door Atticus spoke, "Vera...I..."

"Yeah, Finch?"

"Nothing. It doesn't matter, you won't believe it anyway," as the words left his mouth, Atticus cursed his fearfulness as he watched Vera walk out the door, a single tear running down her cheek.

CHAPTER TEN

Vera got home and ran up to her bedroom. On impulse, she picked up her phone and did the most immature, manipulative thing she could think of…

"Hey, Charles? It's Vera. I was wondering if your offer for a date still stands… It does?... That's great, umm, would you be willing to make that date tonight at the Spring Fling?... Perfect, I'll wait for you at the door at 7:00. Bye!"

Vera quickly hung up the phone and walked over to her closet. She hastily picked out her red cocktail dress. She needed a dress that matched her mood…plus Atticus loved when she wore red. Just the sight of her arm in arm with Charles would make him cringe…add the red dress and his blood was sure to boil. All who knew Vera could tell you that she wasn't vain, but Vera knew she was attractive, and she knew how to use that quality to her advantage.

After putting the finishing touches on her hair and make-up, Vera hurried down the stairs to say goodbye to her parents and show them how she looked. Vera's mom was in the kitchen cooking dinner while her father was playing solitaire in the living room.

"How do I look? I figured red was appropriate for my first dance as a 'grown-up sixteen year old'. It looks more adult."

"You look beautiful, Vera," her mother replied, "Atticus will love you in that dress."

"Speaking of Atticus," Vera's father added, "Where is he? And where are Evan and Ashliana? They're always here for the dances and such."

"Ev and Ash are in Maine this weekend for Ash's great-grand mother's 100th birthday, so they won't be there at all," Vera said intentionally leaving Atticus out of her explanation.

"And Atticus, honey?" her father probed further.

"He's meeting me at the dance," Vera said while trying to hide her bitter disappointment, "I'm taking Charles to the dance."

"Charles? Charles Jenkins? Vera, he's no good for you," her mother said seriously, "Isn't he the boy that always picks on every-one at school? The boy you always prevent from bullying all the other kids in your school? The boy Ashliana calls 'Gaston' and Evan calls 'Prince Humperdinck'?"

"Yes, Mom, but...wait 'Prince Humperdinck'?"

"You know, honey, from the movie *The Princess Bride*?"

"Oh yeah…anyway…he's really not that bad."

"Not that bad? I don't trust that boy, Vera. He has no right tak-ing you to any dance without meeting us first. Why didn't you tell us before?" Mr. Walker asked sternly.

"It just came up, Dad. Atticus decided to take Melyssa Marshall to the dance after I left early from my birthday celebration, so I'm taking Charles. Fair is fair. Plus…I'm a big girl, Dad. I can take care of myself and make my own dating decisions."

"You're sixteen, Vera. You're *far* from being an adult. And besides, honey, did you ever consider that maybe Atticus is tak-ing Melyssa to the dance because he wants to make you *jealous*? Because he doesn't want to lose you? Imagine how you would feel if you planned a special day for Atticus and he bailed on you.

Although you didn't intend to, you probably hurt him very much," Mrs. Walker added.

"No...I actually was too angry at him to think at all at that point. I'm such *an idiot*...I blew things way out of proportion," Vera admitted in a defeated tone.

"You're my best girl, Ver," Mr. Walker said kindly, "You'll figure something out; I just know it. If you don't...well you're not the girl I thought you were."

Vera looked down at her watch. 6:58pm.

"Mom, Dad, I better go wait on the porch for Charles. Don't bother to come out and meet him and take pictures...I need no reminders that this date ever happened."

"No problem, Ver," her dad said half-laughing, "Oh and Ver, I should've asked before, but it slipped my mind. Why are you wearing glasses, honey?"

Quickly racking her brain for an excuse, Vera lied, "It's a new trend, I figured I'd try it. Plus, maybe Charles hates glasses? It might be to my advantage to wear them."

"Whatever you say, honey," Vera's mom said smiling, "Try to have fun. And make up with Atticus; you two have always been there for each other. It would be a shame to throw it all away over a stupid fight."

"Thanks, Mom." Vera checked her watch again. 7:00pm. She opened the door just as Charles pulled up in his car. Begrudgingly, Vera walked down her porch steps towards her date.

"Ready for a fun night, Walker? Hope you brought your dancing shoes!"

"Let's just go to the dance, Charles."

"Fine by me, Walker. Fine by me."

Vera got into the car and Charles sped away from her house. She looked back at her house thinking how much better she would feel if Atticus were the one in the car beside her.

CHAPTER ELEVEN

Vera and Charles walked into the crowded school gymnasium. Before Vera had a chance to prepare herself for the sight of Atticus and Melyssa, the two walked in right behind them. Melyssa looked like what Vera had imagined "Spring Fling Barbie" would look like if she was real; as if a hot-pink princess dress wasn't enough to attract attention, Melyssa also sported an over-sized tiara. Vera was almost positive Atticus was thinking exactly what she was by the way he was awkwardly looking at his date.

Atticus spotted Vera immediately and his jaw dropped. Vera's red dress was simple, yet elegant. It was a low back, halter-top dress with sparkles on the bodice. Vera's make-up made her look like a 1920's movie star and her hair was in a classic French twist. Atticus decided it would only be polite to say hello, so he led Melyssa over to Charles and Vera.

"You look amazing tonight, Ver," Atticus said without thinking.

"Thanks, Atticus. You're wearing your blue shirt. Good choice. It's my favorite," Vera said to Atticus, then turned to Melyssa and remarked, "Your dress suits you, Melyssa." This, of course, was true… only Vera had skillfully added a double meaning to her compliment.

"It does, doesn't it? And it even goes well with my Atti-kissy's shirt," Melyssa said mid-giggle.

"Atti-*kissy*," Vera repeated trying to keep a straight face, "That's *adorable*, Atticus. Too bad I never thought of that one. It's a keeper," Vera added sarcastically.

Charles, getting the impression that Vera could talk to Atticus forever and wouldn't be the first to leave, whether the conversation type be sincere or sarcastic, acted quickly, "Let's dance, Vera."

Vera took his hand out of politeness and was practically dragged onto the dance floor while looking back at Atticus, who promptly got Melyssa to dance as well.

About mid-way through her second dance with Charles, Chelsea Trinity, another of Vera and Atticus's close friends, came over with her boyfriend Kyle Sherwood and politely pulled Vera away to talk with her.

"Vera Eleanor Walker, what on earth are you doing with *Charles Jenkins*? And why the hell is Atticus here with Melyssa 'I can't end a sentence without an obnoxious giggle' Marshall?"

"Long story, Chels…Atticus and I had a misunderstanding."

"Oh, you mean the whole you ditched him in Burlington misunderstanding?" Kyle asked in defense of Atticus, who was one of his best friends.

"It's complicated, Kyle…I explained myself this afternoon…but by then he had already said yes to Melyssa."

"Well, of course, if the girl that I…"

But before Kyle could finish his sentence, Chelsea covered his mouth and spoke over his muffled words.

"What Kyle is trying to say is that Atticus was obviously upset that you left and he probably, in a moment of weakness, said yes to Melyssa because his feelings were hurt."

"I know that *now*, guys, but when I found out about Melyssa earlier I couldn't really think straight. Hence, Charles being my ever-so-charming date."

A muffled sound came from Kyle's mouth and Chelsea, not realizing her hand was still blocking Kyle's speech, removed her hand and mumbled, "Oh, sorry, hun."

All three of them began to laugh. It seemed, with the presence of her friends, that the night was finally starting to pick up, when all of a sudden Charles appeared once again to beckon her to the dance floor. Begrudgingly, Vera followed him turning ever so slightly to throw a miserable look back at her two friends.

About an hour into the dance, Vera began to grow exceedingly bored. Charles was not one for polite or remotely interesting conversation, which were necessities for a girl like Vera.

Atticus, too, found himself wanting to call it a night. Kyle and Chelsea had left so he had no escape routes anymore…and Melyssa's nicknames for him were, throughout the course of the night, becoming more and more gag worthy. As if "Atti-kissy" wasn't enough to make him want to puke, Melyssa had added other nicknames to the list: Atty, Attilicious, and Atty-bear were just a few. Atticus looked over at Vera. He could tell by the look on her face that she was getting annoyed and unbelievably fed up with Charles. She was making her "I'm being fake nice because I'm polite" face. The idea that she was tired of Charles made Atticus swell up with an unexpected feeling of elation. After a few minutes, Atticus figured he would save his friend from death by boredom and made the decision to walk over to see her.

Just as he was making his way to Vera, Charles began to pull her away from the dance floor. Vera turned around hastily, smiled weakly at Atticus, and followed Charles away. Atticus managed a smile then turned around to look for Melyssa, yet in the back of his mind, something was telling Atticus to follow Vera…

"Where are we going, Charles?" Vera asked, nervous for a reason she couldn't put her finger on. For some inexplicable reason her stomach began to twist in discomfort. Oh well, she hadn't eaten in a while…

"Someplace private so we can talk," Charles said calmly, his voice accustomed to his finely spun lies.

"I'd really rather just continue dancing," Vera said faintly, her intuition telling her that following Charles maybe wasn't the best idea.

"No, I think you'll enjoy this."

Enjoy what? Vera needed to know what Charles was up to. She didn't want to get trapped in a situation she couldn't fight her way out of, so she slowly lowered her glasses. At first she heard everyone who was in the same hallway that she and Charles were in. She knew she had to narrow her power down. Maybe if she thought about it hard enough, took control of her gift rather than letting it control her, she could concentrate on just Charles's thoughts. Could it be that simple? It was worth a try at least.

Vera focused on what she wanted. *I am in control. I choose what I hear. I choose when I hear it.* Slowly but surely all the voices went away; Vera heard nothing but her own thoughts. Then Vera looked and focused her attention just on Charles and his thoughts popped out immediately.

*Gotta get away from these people…too many people…need to be alone with her. We have to talk…we **never** talk…she should know how I feel… she should know what I would do…*

Vera quickly turned off the thoughts, excited at the discovery of her talent to control her gift, and continued to follow Charles. If he really did want to have a heart to heart, Vera would prefer to tell him that it wouldn't work out without everyone else around. Vera and Charles slowly turned the corner and entered the boys' locker room. Vera turned "her switch" on to check that they were alone. They were. Vera heard no other thoughts but her own and

Charles's, which were almost identical to his thoughts a few seconds ago. Again, she switched her power off.

"Vera," Charles said slowly, deliberately, yet slightly uncomfortably, "I want to know you," he paused and began to breathe heavily between words and phrases, "Everything about you…all of you… every inch of you- I need to have you, do you understand? I can't keep hiding this anymore!" As he spoke, his voice got angrier, louder, and more crazed, and Vera knew she had a made a mistake following him.

"Charles? Are you okay? You seem…" Vera began to ask nervously, before being cut off.

"I'm *fine*. And now you're here, and I'll finally get to know you, inside and out." His next words came out as half-laughs, the nervous kind that sent shivers up Vera's spine. She had always known Charles to be conceited and rude, but this Charles was different… twisted and frightening. Vera began to back away, and felt her body hit the lockers. She was cornered.

"I would have planned a more romantic venue, but I didn't really have a choice. You see, that idiot Atticus follows you everywhere and, well, I had to jump at this chance. You two seem to have had a bit of a falling out. Trouble in paradise, Vera?"

"Actually we…" Vera began to stammer.

"Don't lie, Vera. You're bad at it. It will only waste my time." Charles said in an eerily collected voice.

"Charles, I'm really sorry, but I just checked the time and… and…I really should be getting home," Vera stuttered nervously trying her best to divert his attention to something else while she moved slowly towards the door, "My parents will worry."

"Oh, Vera. This won't take long. You can go home to Mommy and Daddy as soon as I'm finished," and with his last words, Charles grabbed Vera and pushed her back into the lockers; she fell to the ground with a loud thump.

Vera faced Charles and began to kick at him from the ground, but her legs were no match for his strength. Charles grabbed Vera by the neck and banged her head hard into the lockers, blurring her vision and sending blinding pain through her face and forehead, causing her to fall to the floor. Still, through the pain, Vera continued to kick and struggle as Charles focused his attention on pinning her hands and arms to the ground. In her struggle, Vera could only think of one thing: Atticus. In desperation she screamed for Atticus then, realizing the locker room was soundproof, she began to pray that Atticus could hear her thoughts.

Help me, Atticus! I'm in the boys' locker room...please, help. Atticus, please.

On the dance floor, Atticus was talking with Melyssa when she posed his least favorite fake-sentimental question, "So, what are you thinking of right now?"

Out of nowhere, a strange yet familiar voice began to scream and plead in his head...

Atticus, please, help me. I'm in the boys' locker room...

"Vera-" Atticus said and then his voice trailed off.

"Vera?!" Melyssa asked disgusted, "What do you mean you're thinking about—?"

But Atticus never heard the rest of her sentence, because he was sprinting as fast as he could towards the boys' locker room. He burst through the door, which thanks to Charles's stupidity was unlocked, and threw himself at Charles who was still mid-struggle with Vera. The two began to fight on the ground until Atticus pinned Charles to the floor and began punching him in the face. After just a few punches, Charles's face looked bruised and bloodied and he was out cold; Atticus had just raised his fist for one more swing when an unexpected gentle touch stopped his arm.

"Leave him, Atticus, he's not worth it," Vera said through a plethora of tears, grabbing onto Atticus for comfort and support, "Just take me home...please."

Vera's "please" trailed off and she passed out into her best friend's arms, her head tilted back and her arms limp at her sides. Atticus looked down at Vera. Her French twist was in a complete mess, her lip was bleeding, and she had a bump on her head that was quickly bruising; Vera was right...she needed to get home now. Atticus took Vera into his arms with ease, turned to Charles, and spoke slowly and deliberately to the unconscious body on the floor, "Go to hell."

Then, quickly and carefully, Atticus walked down the hall, across the dance floor through a sea of shocked and confused students, and towards Principal McCormac.

"Atticus!" Melyssa yelled from behind him, "What are you..."

"Not now, Melyssa," he voiced sternly and then, upon reaching the principal, he said point blank, "There's a sick-minded dirt-bag lying on the floor of the boys' locker room. He may need medical attention. I take full responsibility for all his injuries, and before you ask, I'm not sorry. I can explain more later, but right now I have to go."

Principal McCormac opened his mouth and closed it again, as Atticus walked out the gymnasium door and out of the school.

CHAPTER TWELVE

Atticus arrived at the Walker house after walking the one mile from the school with Vera in his arms. He had no car, as he had driven with Melyssa, and, besides, there was something cathartic about walking and taking Vera as far away from Charles as possible. During his walk, Atticus had felt in control of the situation; as long as he held Vera tight and protected her, then everything would be okay.

Without knocking, Atticus maneuvered his hold on Vera and opened the front door. Mr. and Mrs. Walker were sitting in the living room playing Scrabble, and immediately ran over to Atticus, their faces white with fear. Atticus promptly placed Vera on the couch.

"Lynn and Richard...Charles, he...he attacked her. He tried to hurt her...I don't know what's wrong with her. He's disturbed, he disgusting. He's *sick*...he was going to...but, but I stopped him... and then I punched him. Then I brought her here because she told me to, but then she passed out and now I..."

Mrs. Walker put her hands on Atticus's shoulders in a comforting manner and spoke, "Atticus, calm down. You got her here safe. She's going to be okay," and then after a slight pause for thought Mrs. Walker added, "We're going to take her to the hospital now. Would you like to come?" she asked calmly.

"Shouldn't we call an ambulance?" Atticus asked instinctively.

"No...if she wakes up in an ambulance she'll be even more scared, and the hospital is only a five-minute drive from the house. So, do you want to come?"

"Yes. I would," Atticus said finally regaining his cool, his speech eventually finding its proper speed.

On their way to the car, Mrs. Walker looked back at Atticus and, trying to make him smile, said, "Atticus...I can't believe it took an emergency situation for you to call us by our first names. I probably shouldn't get used to it, right?"

Atticus smiled for a second and then looked down at his best friend. Immediately his smile vanished as he looked at Vera's bruised face and bloodied lip. She looked so hurt and helpless; seeing his usually autonomous best friend in such a state terrified Atticus more than anything he'd ever encountered.

"She's going to be okay, Atticus," Mr. Walker said after seeing the young man's face change so rapidly.

"Yeah, I know she is," he replied half-heartedly. Atticus had half a mind to go back to the school and finish beating up Charles. However, he fought this instinct and got into the car next to Vera.

Instinctively, he grabbed Vera's hand and held it tight hoping that she would somehow know that he was with her, watching over her. Just seconds after Atticus took her hand he felt the pressure his hand had given returned to him as Vera's eye lids fluttered open and she stared seriously at Atticus.

"Finch..."

"Hey...how are you feeling?" Atticus asked tenderly rejoicing inside that his friend was conscious.

"I'm sorry, Finch. I was an idiot— all those things I said about you being just another jerk…I was wrong. So wrong. I'm so, so sorry, Atticus."

"Ver, you don't need to apologize. You need to focus on resting," and after a pause, he added, "Are you okay? Did he do anything to you?"

"No…You got there…got there just in time," and Vera paused for second, seeming to focus on forming all her words, "Hey, Atticus?"

"Yeah?"

"Can I lean on your shoulder…it's really comfortable and I want to go to sleep before I see doctors."

"Sure, Ver," Atticus said without hesitation, a smile spreading across his lips, even though he knew "not in shock Vera" would never comment on just how comfortable his shoulder was. However, instead of pressing the matter, Atticus looked down at Vera with a small smile and reaffirmed his previous answer with the words, "Of course you can."

Vera rested her head on Atticus's shoulder, and Atticus rested his head on top of hers gently so as not to cause her any pain. Atticus, although still worried for his friend, found himself feeling happy to just be there in the car with Vera, with her leaning on his shoulder. Within seconds, much to the surprise of Mr. and Mrs. Walker, the two recently incredibly frightened teenagers were fast asleep.

CHAPTER THIRTEEN

Upon reaching the hospital, Atticus quickly realized that, in his effort to keep Vera safe, he had completely forgotten to tell his parents where he was. After fumbling through his pants pocket, Atticus pulled out his phone and dialed his house number.

Mrs. Wells picked up almost immediately and promptly began yelling into the phone at her son; evidently his number had shown up on the caller ID.

"Atticus Jeremy Wells…do you have any idea how worried your father and I have been? I know you're almost sixteen, but by God that does not make you an adult, young man. You are *seriously* mistaken if you think you can go out, miss curfew, and then just call us and expect everything to be fine and dandy, because it's not, Atticus. Your father and I are *so* disappointed in you, and furthermore…"

Aware that Atticus wasn't going to get a word in edgewise, Mr. Walker put his hand out to take the phone and talk to Mrs. Wells. Atticus quickly seized his chance to escape his mother's screams and handed Mr. Walker the phone with force, almost dropping it.

"Hi, Eleanor? Dean? It's Richard Walker. I'm so sorry you worried about Atticus; Lynn and I really should have thought to call you sooner...yes, everything is okay, Vera had a run-in with a boy at the dance...yes, yes she's going to be fine. She's at the hospital right now with all of us, your son included...yes, Atticus is fine too. He was quite the hero tonight, Lynn and I are very thankful he was there to help Vera...yes of course you may talk to him...here he is."

Mr. Walker then passed the phone back to a very grateful-looking Atticus.

"Hey, Mom and Dad...yeah I'm fine, a little shaken up still... Do you mind if I stay here with Vera at the hospital for a while... thanks. Love you both."

Atticus hung up the phone and then walked over to Mr. and Mrs. Walker.

"Is Vera okay to have visitors now? Can I go in and see her?"

Mrs. Walker smiled and replied, "The doctors just came out to tell us that we could go in and see her. Go ahead in."

Atticus walked slowly into Vera's hospital room. He was surprised to find his best friend sitting bolt upright in her hospital bed and looking wide awake...clearly strong pain-killers had no effect on the girl. No sooner had Atticus taken two steps towards the bed, Vera began to talk rapidly: *at him* rather than *to him.*

"Can you believe they're making me spend the night in the hospital? I mean *really*, all I have is a concussion and a sprained wrist. Nothing is even broken! Now I have to stay in this *stupid* bed in this *stupid* room in this *stupid* hospital until the doctor feels satisfied that I'm not gonna die in my sleep or something because of the *stupid* concussion-"

"Vera, you know it's really not bad that they're keeping you here. Your parents and the doctors just want to make sure you're safe. Things could be much worse and—"

Vera cut into Atticus's words with enough sarcasm and frustration for an army. "Things could be much worse, Atticus? *Things could be much worse?* Tell me something, Finch, did *you* get attacked by a per-verted, sex-crazed idiot? Were *you* the one that smashed your head into lockers and then on the floor trying to fight back? Do *you* have a sprained wrist and a concussion? Is *your* beautiful red cocktail dress ripped and ruined? Do *you* have to sleep in the crummy old hospital with all the sick people? And what's more—"

Finally Atticus interrupted in order to defend himself and talk some sense into Vera. "Hold on, Ver, that's enough. No more. I may not be the one with a concussion or a sprained wrist, or a ripped dress but *I am* the guy that was scared to death because tonight I had to rescue my best friend, make sure she wasn't hurt, tell her parents what happened, drive to the hospital, get yelled at by my parents…oh, and here's the winner, Ver: tonight I found out that I can, by some odd coincidence, hear my best friend's thoughts and internal cries for help. So, Ver, before you go postal on me, the person who saved you from the previously mentioned idiot, take a minute and think *for once in your life* before jumping to conclusions."

Vera stared blankly at Atticus for a moment just blinking and not saying anything. Finally, after several seconds, Vera's eyes started to well up with tears. She looked at Atticus with an ex-treme amount of admiration and gratefulness in her eyes and said in a semi-broken voice, "Did I mention that I can never repay you for what you did? Thank you, Atticus. You saved me."

"You're worth saving, Ver. Trust me," Atticus replied as he walked over to Vera and sat down on her hospital bed, "So. How would you like to hear the play-by-play of how my fists owned that stupid idiot?"

"I *was there*, Finch."

"Well…you were kind of out of it, weren't you?"

"Yes, but…"

"So you should hear the story. It's got it all…the villain, the hero, the intense battle scene at the end… "

"Sounds like a story worth hearing. Impress me."

"My friend, have I ever let you down?" Atticus asked with a grin. And then, in the most animated way possible, he relayed the story to Vera.

After the two friends had chatted and joked for a bit, Atticus decided to jump right into the depths of his confusion concerning Vera's rescue.

"Hey, Ver?"

"Yeah," Vera said; her expression changing from happiness to confusion due to the look in Atticus's eyes.

"Well...you may not want to think about this now, but it's kind of important...really important actually, so I was just wondering... if it won't upset you too much...maybe you could, you know-"

"Oh just spit it out, Atticus, while we're both still young."

Atticus tried to carefully plan out his next set of words, but clearly his curiosity and bewilderment concerning the subject deterred his preparation.

"Vera, how on earth did I hear your thoughts in my head? I mean, there I was, just dancing- I was bored mind you but still dancing- with Melyssa and all of a sudden, out of nowhere your voice just appeared in my mind like it belonged there. I know damn well that I can't read minds so I also know *I* didn't make your cry for help appear in my head. It had to be something you did, Ver. Also...where are your glasses?"

Vera looked at Atticus blankly for a number of seconds. She had honestly hoped that they would save this conversation for a different day, but at the same time she knew that Atticus would never let something like hearing her voice in his head go...the fact that she learned to control her powers without the glasses had also slipped her mind...

"Okay, I'll answer the easy question first. I was bored hanging with Charles, plus he was starting to creep me out, so I decided to take my glasses off to hear what he was thinking...you know make sure he was safe to be around. Well, needless to say, that back-fired, but I was able to somehow make myself hear only Charles's thoughts and then turn the thoughts off all together. I don't know how I was able to control the thoughts so quickly...maybe I needed a sense of urgency to trigger it?"

"That makes sense...as much sense as possible in this situation...Can you turn them back on?"

"The thoughts?"

"Yeah."

"Umm...I don't know. Let me check."

Vera focused in on Atticus, and almost instantaneously she began to get an influx of his thoughts...

*Aww man...not my thoughts again. This didn't end well last time for me...maybe if I just try to clear my head, think of nothing. Okay, clearing-clearing-clearing...Vera still likes me, and I rescued her. That was pretty awesome...**I'm** pretty awesome. I totally punched that guy right in the face and showed him who was boss. I mean, my hands **really hurt** right now, but who cares? I owned him...I showed him who's allowed to be with Vera and...damn. Hey, Ver? You still listening?*

"Yep, the whole time, and you know what I think?" Vera's next few words came out as clear teases, "Atticus, I think you're awesome. Like, you're *so* awesome. Did I tell you that you were *awesome*?"

"So, yeah, you did hear my thoughts...all of them apparently."

"I did...so, in all seriousness, do you need to get your hands checked out?"

"Nah, they made sure nothing was broken and bandaged me up just fine before I came in to see you. See," Atticus said holding up his hands for Vera to inspect, "I'll be good as new in no time."

"Good. Now that I know that that's taken care of, and that I've still got my mind-reading mojo, let's try to figure out question number two."

"Fair enough...continue the story and let's see what we can figure out."

60

"Right. After I read Charles's mind, which was *very* unhelpful by the way, I followed him into the boys' locker room because he said he wanted to talk."

"Wanted to talk...right."

"Come on, Finch. We all know the end; you don't have to rub it in."

"*Fine.* Continue."

"Charles started talking. And at first he was fine. I mean he just sounded upset, but then his voice started to sound scary and dangerous...that's when I knew I had made a mistake. I've never heard him sound so...I can't describe it, Finch. It was surreal. Before I could even think of an escape plan he grabbed me and threw me...and—" Vera paused here, evidently still upset by the night's events.

Atticus immediately noticed his friend's discomfort, "Ver, you don't need to tell me everything, you know. I would never force you to do that."

"I know you wouldn't, Atticus, but I have to tell you. I can't just pretend it didn't happen at all," Vera snapped back at Atticus.

"Okay, okay, no need to get all defensive. Go ahead and finish the story."

"I was fighting him off, but he was so much stronger than me... All I could think of was that if you were around, you could help me, you know? So I just asked for your help in my head. I thought it was useless to be honest but it obviously worked."

The two looked at each other for a while. Finally, Atticus spoke, "Ver, maybe your power is more complicated than we thought it was. I was thinking...you can read other people's thoughts, so in a way it's like they're giving thoughts to you- even though they don't know it- and it only makes sense that you should be able to give your thoughts back to people. Maybe you can- I don't know- *throw* your thoughts at people?"

"*Throw* my thoughts, Atticus? That's ridiculous."

"Do you have a better explanation? Plus, a week ago you would have said that reading people's minds was quote unquote ridiculous. Try it now. Throw your thoughts to me."

"*Come on*, Atticus. It makes no sense."

"Ver, it is literally the only halfway reasonable explanation for how I was able to find you and rescue you tonight," and then Atticus sternly added, "Try it, Ver. Don't be closed-minded. Trust me."

"Fine...if it will make you happy."

"It will."

Vera began to concentrate. No sooner had she put her mind to the seemingly impossible task of "throwing her thoughts," Atticus was bombarded by Vera's loud voice in his head once again.

God this is so childish, Atticus. You're being a big losermuffin.

"Losermuffin, Ver? Who on earth uses 'losermuffin' as an insult? "

Vera looked at Atticus stunned, "You *heard* that?"

"Well, yeah. *I* didn't come up with losermuffin. I'm serious, where did you pick up that gem of an insult?"

Vera looked down at her hands and smiled, slightly embarrassed, and answered with a laugh, "Ben and Bastian."

"Wow. I would comment more, and believe me later I will make it my goal to tease you endlessly, but now it is exactly 1:06 am and you, my losermuffin friend, need to get some rest."

Atticus got up off the bed and began to walk towards the door.

"Hey, Finch?"

"Yeah?"

"I was just wondering...and I'm not scared or anything...you know I'm completely self-sufficient and I can totally take care of myself, but..."

"I'll stay here until you fall asleep, Ver."

"Thanks, Finch," Vera said yawning, the excitement of her night finally catching up with her.

Atticus sat down in the chair directly to Vera's right. Once he got as comfortable as humanly possible, he looked over at Vera, who seemed to be almost asleep. Not wanting to wake her, he closed his eyes to try to sleep.

Vera's voice startled him even though it was small and quiet. "Goodnight, Atticus...I love you," and then she drifted off into sleep, breathing slowly in and out.

Atticus looked at his friend and, even though she couldn't hear him, he whispered, "I love you too, losermuffin," and smiled to himself.

CHAPTER FOURTEEN

The next week at school was like a whirlwind for Vera and Atticus. Every corner the two turned seemed to contain a group of their classmates dying to be told the whole story of Vera's close-call and Atticus's daring rescue. The only people they actually graced with the entire story sans the mind reading were Evan, Ashliana, Kyle, and Chelsea.

Atticus had never been more popular in his entire life than in the week after he rescued Vera. Every girl in school wanted to talk to him. Every guy either wanted to be his friend or hated him (because he was inadvertently stealing attention). He was asked out on dates by every member of the cheerleading squad, and the student council members approached him about speaking on his experience as a means of educating others to take a stand against violence. To most high school kids, this would have been a dream...but for Atticus it was just plain annoying.

Vera was tired of talking about the subject of her attack- it was as simple as that. All she cared about was that Charles's family had sent him to military school after the incident (the court couldn't do much as he was a minor with no previous criminal record). Charles was far away from her and had to stay far away from her legally as she had also procured a restraining order against him.

Truthfully speaking, Vera was somewhat jealous of Atticus's sudden popularity. Granted she had always been well-liked, and so had Atticus, but she couldn't help feeling slightly afraid that Atticus might decide to leave her behind for his newer and cooler friends. Of course, she knew this fear was ridiculous, but it was there nonetheless, always nagging at her. When Vera decided to tell Ashliana, Evan, and Kyle about her worries, they laughed.

"It's not funny, guys!"

"Vera," Kyle said, looking her square in the eyes, "You seriously think that Atticus, *Atticus* is going to ditch you?"

"Well, I don't know. It's high school…things happen sometimes."

"Don't be an idiot, Vera," Kyle's girlfriend Chelsea said, seemingly coming out of nowhere.

"That's easy for you to say, Chels. You're perfect."

"I resent that, Vera Walker. Being perfect would make me boring."

"And Chelsea here," Ashliana added putting her arm around Vera and gesturing towards Chelsea, "Is certainly not boring."

"I know that, Ash, but don't you think it makes sense for me to worry a little?"

"Will the whining never cease? Vera, 'Finch' isn't gonna ditch you. The guy is my best friend and he's completely in love with you so there's no reason to worry," Evan said spontaneously without giving his words much thought.

"Subtle, Ev. Nice work," Kyle said staring at Evan like he had said something blasphemous.

"Atticus…is in love…*with me?*" Vera asked more dumbfounded than her friends could have expected.

"Oh come on, Ver. The guy thinks you're the greatest thing since sliced bread," Kyle said, seeing no harm in further discussing the topic since it was now out in the air.

"He's always there to help you," Ashliana added.

"Because he's my best friend," Vera said as a retort.

"He knows exactly what you like and don't like. The guy can practically read your mind...it's *creepy*," Evan said with an over-exaggerated face of sarcastic terror.

Vera chose to brush over the mind-reading comment and said in reply, "Because we've known each other for years and years."

"He thinks all your annoying OCD-like tendencies are endearing," Chelsea said with a knowing look.

"Because he knows I put up with his quirks too...and I am not OC—"

"And," Evan said interrupting her, "He gets all excited and nervous when you come to see our soccer games."

"That," Vera said adamantly, "Is just 'before game nerves'."

"Yeah...okay," Kyle said his voice dripping with mockery, "I only ever got that nervous for a hockey game when Chelsea came to watch me play before we started dating and I had a huge crush on her. There's a big difference between pre-game jitters, and wanting to impress someone so much that you can't think straight."

"Come on, guys," Vera said rolling her eyes, "It's Atticus. We've been best friends since pre-school. He's like, you know..."

"You say the words 'my brother' and, Vera, I swear to God I am putting you in an institution," Ashliana said exasperatedly.

"Well whatever he is...he is my best friend and it wouldn't work."

"Best friends become couples all the time," Ashliana continued, "Take Evan and I for example."

"N-n-n-n-no. Ash, you *hated* Evan in elementary school *and* in middle school. He used to stick your hair in the paints and call you names on the playground!"

"Her hair looked prettier with blue in it!"

"Awww…thanks, babe," Ashliana said sarcastically.

"Oh shut up, the both of you!"

"And you," Vera continued rounding on Kyle, "You never even spoke to Chelsea until I introduced you after she and I had our figure skating show!"

"I was nervous!"

"So, the two of you weren't *friends first.*"

"No," Chelsea said, "But just because our relationships didn't start as friends first, doesn't mean your relationship can't. Gosh, Ver, stop with the lectures."

Vera stared at her friends for what seemed, to the others, to be hours and then asked, "How long have you guys felt this way? About me and Atticus I mean."

"It's not how we feel, Ver," Evan said finally in a serious tone, "You two just…*fit.*"

"Who fits?" Atticus's voice came from behind the group and made everyone jump.

"You know…Ron and Hermione from *Harry Potter* AND Arwen and Aragorn from *The Lord of the Rings* AND Meg Murry and Calvin O'Keefe from *A Wrinkle in Time.* They're FRIENDS FIRST and then they get together at the end," Chelsea said simply giving Vera a strange look.

"Am I missing something here?" Atticus said turning to Vera.

"Nope…we were just talking books. Same old same old," Vera said entirely too quickly to be convincing.

"O…kay," Atticus said looking at Evan as if to beg the question, *what the hell is going on?*

"Annnnnd, we're gonna be late for class," Ashliana said to clear the air.

"Yeah," Kyle agreed, "We should get going. We can't be late just to fill Atticus in about *Ron and Hermione.*"

"Alrighty then, let's go!" Vera said in a peppy, yet bothered tone.

On the way to class, Atticus couldn't help but think that he had missed something much more important than the discussion of the romantic relationship of fictional characters.

⊰⊱

When Friday finally came, Vera and Atticus were thrilled to have a weekend without the constant bombarding questions and requests for information. The two were especially excited because it was Benedict and Sebastian's birthday. Vera and Atticus were told to meet the boys outside their school and walk them home; the boys loved when Atticus came with Vera to walk with them: it was a "special treat" for the two of them.

By the time the school bell rang later that day, Vera and Atticus were just about ready to burst with the knowledge of their happiness to finally get a break from their classmates and their ongoing questions. They grabbed their books quickly and hastened out the school building.

Just as Vera and Atticus were approaching the elementary school to meet the boys, Vera received a phone call from her mother.

"Vera?" Mrs. Walker asked frantically.

"What is it, Mom? Why do you sound so upset? Is everything okay?"

"Honey, your brothers are missing. They had extra recess today because of the nice weather and when the kids lined up to go back inside and get their things Ben and Bastian weren't there. No one has seen them anywhere, and you know they never wander off by themselves…Vera, I don't…I can't…what am I supposed to…" Mrs. Walker's last few words came out as sobs.

"Mom…listen to me. You called the police right?"

"Yeah…I called."

"Okay then. Atticus and I are going to do a huge search okay? It's going to be okay, Mom. I promise."

Vera hung up the phone and looked up at Atticus. Her eyes looked terrified as she filled Atticus in on the situation.

"My brothers are missing, Finch. No one can find them. They didn't come in from afternoon recess...Atticus, what if someone took them? What if they're hurt?"

"Listen to me, Vera. We're going to do exactly what you said we were going to do. We're going to find them, Ver, you hear me? We are going to find them. They're going to be okay. Now let's go search the area near the school. They might be there."

"Right," Vera said, more to reassure herself than Atticus.

The two ran quickly towards the school. When they got there, Vera began looking around frantically, not really paying any attention to what she was doing.

"Vera...*Vera!* You need to calm down if we're going to find them. We need to think for a second. What are all the possible places that your brothers might like to explore? They could have wandered off and gotten lost."

"That's just it...Ben and Bastian never wander off, Atticus. They never do anything without asking first. They are annoyingly well-behaved to a fault," Vera said adamantly and harshly.

"Alright, alright, I'm just trying to brainstorm. Wait...Ver, why don't you try to find their thoughts? Concentrate on finding just *their* thoughts. Maybe if you can pinpoint their thoughts, that will give us an idea of where they are!"

"Atticus, I've only ever read people's thoughts when they were in close proximity to me...I don't even know if I can read from far away!"

"A week ago you didn't think you could throw thoughts either and you did that when you needed to. Just try, Ver, okay? What's it going to hurt to try?"

"I can't. It won't work...I'm not strong enough."

"It will work. *Just trust me.* You can do that right?"

"Of course I can," Vera replied faintly before guarding herself and saying, "Fine. I'll try." Vera closed her eyes and tried to focus on Ben and Bastian's thoughts. At first nothing happened, but then suddenly she could hear them. First she heard Ben:

I should never have followed Bastian…he always gets us in trouble with Mom and Dad and now we're lost in the woods and I'm scared and I want to go home. What if we get stuck here in the dark with no place to sleep but the ground? What if we're lost for good and no one ever finds us?

Soon after, Bastian's thoughts came into the picture:

Ben is being such a baby…I keep telling him that the woods behind the playground can't go on forever…there has to be an opening somewhere, right? I mean, the woods have an end…we're just on a little adventure… that's all. I do wish Dad was with us though…

"They're in the woods behind the playground…I don't know where exactly, but I know they're in there somewhere! I did it, Atticus!"

"Of course you did!" Atticus said hugging Vera, "Now, come on, let's search the woods!"

Vera and Atticus ran into the woods and began to search diligently for the boys. The two took turns calling their names and listening for any reply. After searching the woods for a little over an hour, Vera was just about ready to cry.

"Maybe I was wrong. Maybe they're not here, Finch. We've searched everywhere…it's getting dark."

"You're wrong, Ver. They're here. *You heard them.* We just have to look a little harder. Call their names one more time, Ver."

"What's the point, Atticus?" And Vera leaned her back against the nearest tree for stability and began a vain attempt at trying to muffle her oncoming sobs. Vera had literally gone from a sensible, mature teenager to a miserable ball of mush in seconds; she had always been there to protect her brothers, and now she was failing them. The thought of losing them made Vera feel helpless and small.

"*I'll* call their names then," Atticus said in a strong voice hoping to give his friend some strength and hope, "Ben?!?! Bastian?!?! Are you out there? Ben and Bastian Walker?!?! Can you hear me? It's Atticus and Vera!"

Initially there seemed to be no response, but then, out of nowhere, two small voices were heard in the distance.

"Finch?"

"Vera?"

Vera heard the voices right when Atticus did and looked up at him. Atticus reached his hand out to pull her away from the tree.

"Let's bring them home, Ver. Alright boys, just keep yelling to me so I can hear where your voices are coming from!"

And after only five minutes of yelling from both parties, Atticus and Vera finally spotted Ben and Bastian who were running desperately fast towards them. When the boys reached Vera and Atticus they instinctually ran into the relieved looking teenagers and began hugging them.

"You found us!" Ben said excited and relieved.

"We thought we were going to have to sleep in the woods!" added Bastian.

"Did you really think we were going to let you guys have a fun camping adventure without us? I, Atticus Jeremy Wells, would never stand for such nonsense, and neither would your sister!" The boys began to laugh hysterically before looking up at their sister.

"Vera, why are you crying? It's okay...we're fine, see?" Ben said, trying to make his sister feel better.

"I'm just crying because I'm so happy we found you, Let's go home," Vera said calmly finally able to speak.

Bastian took Atticus's hand and Ben took Vera's and they all began to walk home. Vera passed Ben her phone.

"Call Mom, Ben. Tell her all four of us are coming home."

As the four of them continued to walk, Vera looked down at Atticus's open hand, thought about the conversation she'd had with her friends earlier in the week, and took it in hers. Atticus looked down surprised, then up at Vera and smiled.

"Hey Mommy, it's Ben! We're coming home!"

CHAPTER FIFTEEN

When Atticus, Vera, Ben, and Bastian got home they were surrounded first by Mr. and Mrs. Walker, and then by several police officers and detectives. The twins were allowed to go and eat dinner, but Vera and Atticus were required to stay behind to talk to the police. After what seemed like a million years of questioning, writing, and reporting, the officers and detectives finally left the house.

Mr. and Mrs. Walker both looked down at Benedict and Sebastian with faces filled with a mix of relief, anger, disappointment, and exhaustion. Mr. Walker spoke first.

"Boys, you know better than to wander into the woods, or to wander off anywhere by yourselves. Why on earth would you do such a thing? Your mother and I raised the two of you to be more careful than that. What if Vera and Atticus hadn't found you? What if someone had come and taken you away from us forever?"

"We're sorry, Dad," Ben replied.

"Yeah. The only reason we went into the woods was because we saw a man," added Bastian.

"Yeah! You've gotta believe him…he's telling the truth! There was a man in the trees! He looked familiar but we couldn't see his face clearly so we followed him to try to figure out who he was," Ben said very matter-of-factly.

"We think he saw us following because he started to run. We ran after him, but we never caught him," Bastian said defeated.

"Yep, and then we got lost," said Ben ending their short explanation.

Mrs. Walker looked down at her boys and frowned.

"Are you saying that you boys followed a stranger into the woods? What has Mommy told you about strangers?"

"But he wasn't a stranger, Mom! Bastian and I *knew* him. We just needed a better look, which was hard to get because he was wearing greenish clothes…"

"Boys," Mr. Walker said sternly, "Whether you recognized the man or not, you should never have wandered into those woods on your own."

"What did this man look like again, boys?" Vera asked sounding slightly on edge.

"We already told you, Ver," Bastian said, "We recognized him but we don't know from where."

"Well was he young? Old? Tall? Short? Skinny? Fat? What color hair? What color eyes? Did he look menacing?"

"Vera, why in the world are you asking the boys all these questions?" asked Mrs. Walker very confused while Atticus gave her a concerned look, "Don't encourage them, please, Vera. Boys, wash up and go to sleep. We'll do your birthday stuff tomorrow."

"Aww, Mom," both boys said in unison.

"No 'aww Moms'; now go."

"You believe us about the man, right Mom and Dad?" the boys said almost in unison.

"Yes, boys, but that doesn't make us not want you in bed. Upstairs… come on, the both of you."

"Fine," Sebastian said disappointed.

Ben stayed downstairs just long enough to talk with Vera and Atticus.

"The man was tall and he had big muscles. I couldn't see his eyes, but he had blonde hair. He wasn't very young, but he didn't look *old*. I don't know, Ver. We didn't get a good look."

"Benedict," his father's voice scolded, "Get up to your room right this instant!"

"Yes, Dad. Goodnight, Vera. Goodnight, Finch. Thanks for finding us," Ben said before walking up the stairs.

"Yeah, thanks!" Sebastian yelled down after him.

"We'd never make our favorite boys sleep in the woods!" Atticus yelled, invoking laughter in the twins. After the laughter died down, he turned to Vera, "Why the obsession with the man in the woods?" he asked.

Vera paused for a moment and then spoke.

"I'm just being paranoid, Finch, that's all. Let's go find my parents in the kitchen. I'm starving."

Something about the way Vera had spoken made Atticus feel on edge, but considering his hunger, he decided to drop the subject for the time being and quickly followed Vera into the kitchen.

CHAPTER SIXTEEN

When Vera and Atticus arrived in the kitchen, food was already set on the table for them. All Mr. and Mrs. Walker had time to make during the crisis was spaghetti, but to both Vera and Atticus, who were ravenous, the meal might as well have been the best meal they had ever eaten. After the two of them had practically inhaled their food, they walked into the living room and sat down with Vera's parents. At first everyone in the room was silent...the type of silence that irked Vera. She knew something was up with her parents so she asked the obvious question that was hanging in the air.

"Mom? Dad? Is everything okay?"

Mr. Walker spoke first, "Before we say anything, we both want you and Atticus to know how much we appreciate the both of you. You saved the boys today. The two of you kept looking when the rest of us were losing hope."

Vera suddenly felt compelled to confess her own doubts, "Mom and Dad...to tell you the truth, I almost gave up too. I was so scared,

I froze...it's like I couldn't think. Atticus was the one that kept the two of us going. He was *amazing*."

Feeling slightly embarrassed, Atticus added, "It was nothing, really. Vera just needed a little boost of optimism. We made a great team."

"In any case," Mr. Walker said more sternly than expected, "thank you again."

Another awkward silence followed which put even easy-going Atticus on edge. Something was up that the Walkers weren't telling them. Finally, after what seemed like forever to the two friends, Mrs. Walker spoke in a calm yet deliberate voice to the both of them.

"How did the two of you find the boys?" she asked in a tone that implied suspicion.

Atticus spoke first as he knew Vera was a horrible liar. "Well," he said trying to remain composed, "We both saw the woods behind the school, and I was talking to Vera about how when I was eleven, I totally would have wanted to explore those woods...I mean, what little kid doesn't want to explore, right? It was the perfect place to look. At first Vera didn't believe me because she said the boys never went off on their own because they were old enough to know better, but seriously kids slip up sometimes, you know what I mean? It just makes sense," and with that Atticus finally ended his poorly crafted lie.

"And nothing else gave you a hint as to the woods?" Mr. Walker asked.

Atticus continued, this time with his thoughts more collected, "We did some detective work. Like, we both put our heads together and realized that because the boys were at recess, they only had a few seconds, a minute tops, to disappear from the view of the teachers-"

Vera quickly went along with this new and better lie to make the story look more convincing, "Yeah, so that means they had to have gone missing or gotten lost or disappeared someplace near the school. I mean, seriously, recess is only twenty minutes in the afternoon," and then she added the frosting on the top of the lie cake, "We were totally like Sherlock Holmes and Watson, Mom and Dad!"

Mr. and Mrs. Walker looked at the two teenagers for a while and then walked over and hugged them both. Mrs. Walker began to talk through tears, "We're so...so sorry we're questioning you. It's just...it's a miracle you found them in those woods. We are so blessed to have both of you. You're our best girl, Vera. And Atticus...you're...you're...we love you so much!"

"We love you too; we know you've been through a lot today. I don't know what I would have done if Atticus and I hadn't found them. I can't even think about it without cringing."

"You're like my second family. I would do anything for you guys. Plus, I don't have any brothers and sisters of my own...the boys might as well be my brothers too," Atticus said with a smile.

"Maybe you and Dad should get some rest, Mom. You two look exhausted. Atticus and I won't be up for much longer; don't worry about us. We'll finish the dishes and everything."

"You two are so sweet. We love you," Mrs. Walker said, finally getting a hold of herself.

"Goodnight, kids. Don't stay up too late," Mr. Walker said before walking upstairs with his wife.

"We won't, Dad. I promise," Vera said, taking Atticus's hand and leading him into the kitchen. The two of them quickly began to clean up the small amount of dishes and put them away...oddly, neither of them spoke as they were at a strange loss as to what to say to one another. As they were about to finish putting away the last dishes, Atticus finally tried to begin a conversation.

"Why do you think your parents were giving us the old Q and A? It was like being interrogated by the police," Atticus said while putting away a dish Vera had just handed to him.

"I don't know," Vera said, her voice almost devoid of emotion.

"That's it? You don't know? Do you think they could know something? You know, about your Jedi mind tricks?"

"They can't…it's not possible, I mean, how could they, right?"

"Right. Of course. It must have been their worry and exhaustion talking," Atticus replied after noting Vera's rise in nervousness, "Anyway…it's late so I should probably go and let you get some rest."

"Yeah…right, that makes sense. I'll walk you out," Vera said trying to hide the disappointment in her voice.

The two walked out the front door; as Atticus began to walk down the steps he felt Vera's hand on his shoulder, "Wait…can I, ummm, talk to you for a second? We could sit on the porch swing?"

"Yeah…sure, I guess I could stay for a few more minutes. My parents can't possibly ground me for being a little late after I helped rescue the twins."

They both sat down on the porch swing, and Vera again grabbed Atticus's hand and held it. Atticus seemed surprised, but not unhappy, which Vera took as a good sign. The two sat there for a few moments without saying a word until Vera couldn't take it anymore.

"You saved me again today, Atticus."

"What do you mean?" he replied, slightly confused.

"I had a total meltdown in the woods when I thought we wouldn't find the boys, and you just kept looking even though I could tell you were nervous too. You had to be strong for both of us…and then just now…you totally covered for my new weird brain powers without even thinking twice. You're the hero of the day Atticus, not me."

"Vera, you didn't have a total meltdown. Your brothers were missing and you were worried. And I think you're forgetting that without your so called 'weird brain powers' we wouldn't have found the boys in the first place."

Even though Vera knew this, her next words came out as half yells and her eyes began to glisten as if about to tear, "But even with my powers you had to be the strong one. You had to pick up *my* slack! I hate being vulnerable, Atticus…I hate having to depend on people. I've been such a mess lately and all I want to do is keep being the independent girl I want to be, but I can't…it's *killing* me. I don't want to have to need people…but lately I *can't help* but need people. Mostly, I can't help but need *you*, and to tell you the truth, that terrifies me because we both know that I pride myself on being able to stand on my own and take care of myself… because God only knows my mom and dad need to take care of the boys, and as today illustrated they're certainly a handful to say the least. So you know, I'm kind of used to being on my own, taking care of myself…no questions asked, you know? And now—"

But she never got to finish her sentence, because Atticus had lowered his face to Vera's, cupped her face in his hands and kissed her suddenly, making her heart leap and welcome chills run up her spine and around her shoulders and neck. When the two broke apart, Vera looked up at Atticus who was grinning widely.

"Wow, after eleven years I've finally figured how stop your incessant, animated, wordy diatribes," he said mid-laugh, "Who knew it was that easy?"

Vera gave a half laugh and, with a sudden movement, threw her arms around Atticus's neck, and responded, "Took you long enough, losermuffin," before kissing him back.

CHAPTER SEVENTEEN

Atticus woke up the next day and smiled remembering the events of the night before. He and Vera had rescued the twins, gone home, talked with Vera's parents, done the dishes, and then walked onto the porch...and on the porch he and Vera had kissed. After that, they talked for a few more minutes until Vera was tired and, like a gentleman, Atticus walked her to the front door, kissed her goodnight, and then walked the two minutes it took him to get home.

Today felt like the beginning of a new era for Atticus; he was finally dating the girl that he had been in love with since puberty. Atticus was well aware that not many fifteen year olds could say that they truly loved someone...but he could. As much as it could be embarrassing for a teenage boy to admit, Atticus loved Vera- at her best and at her worst. Today he and Vera would go on their first official date; Atticus was thrilled.

Vera woke up feeling more rejuvenated and happy than she had felt in a long, long time. Finally the puzzle pieces of her life were all coming together. Amazing family? Check. Good friends?

Check. Excellent grades? Check. Powers under control? Check. Boyfriend and best friend all in one? *Check.* She smiled widely at the last realization.

Vera sat bolt upright in her bed. She went over to her radio and turned it on. This type of mood, according to Vera, needed great music to go with it. As if on cue, Michael Buble's "Everything" came on the radio.

"Perfect," Vera said to herself and began to dance around in her room and get ready for her first date ever with Atticus.

Vera had been on a lot of dates before, but never one where she really *knew* the person she was going out with. Usually dates meant a small dinner somewhere or a trip to the movies. The conversation usually consisted of small talk or normal introductory remarks; with Atticus a date would be much different.

Atticus already knew her favorite book, favorite movie, favorite place to vacation, favorite food, favorite candy, favorite ice cream flavor…He also knew all her weaknesses: a fact that made Vera incredibly uneasy…

Mid-way through his nostalgic day-dreaming about "the perfect date with Vera," Atticus realized that he had no clue what he was going to talk to her about. He and Vera had talked everyday non-stop since the day they met; the two never tired of conversing. Why then was his mind blanking on what he was going to talk to her about today?

He couldn't worry about this. First off, he didn't have time as he had to meet Vera at her house in twenty minutes so he needed to spend his energy getting ready. Secondly, it was *Vera*. He knew Vera, so why should he be nervous? They always had plenty to talk about…actually, to be honest, most days he couldn't get her to stop talking if his life depended on it.

Everything was going to be fine.

Vera put the finishing touches on her make-up (just a small amount, as usual), turned off her radio, left her room, and walked down the stairs toward the front door. As if on cue, the doorbell rang. Vera opened the door to a smiling Atticus who was holding a bag of salt and vinegar potato chips in his hand.

"Hey," Vera said more shyly than she expected.

"Hey."

"What's with the chips?" Vera asked, a confused expression on her face.

"Oh, these," Atticus said amidst nervous laughter, "Well, I know you don't like the whole 'guy gives girl flowers at the door thing,' so I decided to bring you your favorite chips instead. Why you like this kind is beyond me, but hey I figure to each his own...or her own in your case...anyway, here."

Atticus handed the chips to Vera with one quick, uneasy motion.

"These are perfect, Atticus," Vera said smiling, realizing how much she had worried for nothing.

At her words Atticus relaxed, took Vera's hand, and led her out the door for a "re-do" birthday date in Burlington.

CHAPTER EIGHTEEN

Vera and Atticus got off the bus quickly and began to go through the motions of their make-up "Vera's Birthday" date in Burlington. The two went back to Uncommon Grounds again, then to Bove's, and then to Ben & Jerry's. Vera insisted that Atticus refrain from buying her another five books as he would be spoiling her if her did, and instead bought Atticus a soccer ball and a pair of goalie gloves he had wanted for a while.

After the two of them had annihilated their spending money (most of which went toward both Barnes & Noble and F.Y.E), Vera assumed that they would be catching the 3:30pm bus back home. However, it seemed Atticus had other plans.

"Hey, Ver...How would you like to take a trip to the Fletcher Free Library? You know, the one on College Street?"

"Sure, Finch, I guess so. Why?"

"I know how important it is for you to 'be in the loop,' especially when it concerns *your* life. I can tell you're confused about your gift still, and believe me I don't blame you. I figured if we did some digging in the library about our town history maybe something would pop up that might give us a clue about your powers."

"Finch, you are honestly going to spend your Saturday night in a library with me looking up *town history*?"

Atticus looked at Vera confused by her expression, "Yeah, well, that was my plan. Unless you don't want to of course."

"No, Finch, I do want to...it's just...you're spending so much time trying to help me figure out all my problems and you're completely cool with it."

"And?"

"And it's strange. *Nice*...but strange. Not many people can say that they have friends who would do that for them."

"Well, you and I aren't quite normal are we?" Atticus asked before kissing Vera, taking her breath away.

"No...we're not," Vera said smiling once they stopped kissing.

"So, what do you say? Do you want to head over to College Street?"

"I do," Vera replied and the two of them began their trek to the Fletcher Free Library.

❧

Vera and Atticus walked up the library stairs and through the doors. Atticus quickly approached the front desk to speak to the librarian.

"Excuse me, but do you know where I can find books on the history of Seckerlyn Center?"

"Take a left and the stacks in the back should have the books you're looking for," the librarian responded kindly.

"Thank you," Atticus replied politely, and then led Vera towards the old bookcase in the back.

"What exactly are we looking for, Finch?"

"I'm not sure...but just to be safe, maybe we should try the whole mind conversation thing here. We may cause a disturbance if we constantly mention the fact that you can read minds," Atticus said sternly in a whisper.

"Right. Good idea."

Shall we start now?
> *Sounds good to me.*
Wow, this actually works.
> *Yeah, it's pretty cool...but for time's sake we probably shouldn't dwell on it.*
Fair enough...let's do this.

⊱⋅ ⋅⊰

After about an hour, Vera and Atticus thought they must have searched through all of the historical records about Seckerlyn Center in existence, and the two were getting very, very annoyed and bored.

We've searched everywhere, Atticus, and still nothing. Maybe I'm the only weirdo in Seckerlyn existence.
> *You're not a weirdo, Ver... There must be something we're missing...oooo, how about this? <u>Legends and Folklore: Seckerlyn Center</u>. This looks promising, Ver.*
I saw that already, Finch. It's just a bunch of myths and ghost stories. I wouldn't bother.
> *You wouldn't bother? Ver, I know you're not into the whole idea of magic and the paranormal and the supernatural, but you of all people should be open to checking this book out! I mean, you're like the poster child for weird right now...no offense.*
I know, Finch, but that book? Really? You honestly think there's something in that book that can help us?

Never judge a book by its cover, Ver.

Haha, Atticus.

Seriously, let's at least take a look at it...it can't hurt to look.

Fine. If you insist.

Ver, check it out...there's a whole chapter on telepaths!

Telepaths?

Yeah, you know, people blessed with powers of telepathy? People who can read minds? Just follow along in my head while I read it. It says, since the founding of Seckerlyn Center in 1845, there have been numerous accounts of people claiming to be telepathic. All of these suspected telepaths have been women, and all are blood relatives of Ella Promur, Seckerlyn Center's first recorded telepath.

Who's Ella Promur?

How am I supposed to know? This is the first time I've heard her name too.

Keep reading, Finch.

Right. There's something here about some woman who could move things with her mind...wow that's pretty impressive...

Atticus!?!?

Patience is a virtue, Ver...found it! Ella Promur married a man named Christian Paulsen in 1850 when she was only eighteen. The two lived happily in Seckerlyn Center for their whole lives and Ella bore Christian four children: three boys Aidan, Ronan, and Gerard, and one girl, their eldest child, Maura. In the year 1868, on the eve of her sixteenth birthday, Maura Paulsen was deemed a telepath, a fact which was recorded in the town census report.

Maura was sixteen when she got her powers?

I guess so, Ver. Should I continue?

Yes, of course!

Okay...Maura Paulsen married John Campbell in 1872. Maura bore John twins, a son Marcus and a daughter Evelynn...

Again, when Evelynn Campbell turned 16 in 1890 she was reg-
istered as a telepath.
This is so bizarre. Can you give me a speed through of the rest of
the lineage.
Yeah…so Evelynn Campbell married Zachary Taylor in 1894,
they had one child, Maeve in 1896. Maeve Taylor got her pow-
ers in 1912, and later married William Kelly in 1916. The
two had five children: four boys Cameron, Daniel, Jacob, and
Aaron and one girl Lexy, but…
But what, Atticus?
The lineage keeps going, but no more women were registered as
telepaths. In 1918, when Lexy was two, the registry shut down
for an unidentified reason.
Probably because registering people is ridiculous.
Agreed. Anyway, the last recorded family member written in
this book is Lexy's daughter Rachel (Moran) Reilly, born in
1936. If she's alive, Rachel would be seventy-one right now.
Do you think there's a way we can find her? Atticus, what if Rachel
Reilly is my grandmother?
It certainly seems like a valid possibility to me. It's definitely
worth checking out.
Hey, Finch? Do you mind if we talk out loud now? My head is get-
ting very tired.
Yeah, of course, Ver…that's fine.

"What do you say we ask the librarian if she knows anything
about Rachel Reilly?"
"The librarian? Really, Ver?"
"Oh, come on, you never know!"
"Alright. Let's go."
Vera decided she wanted to be the one to ask the librarian
about Rachel Reilly, her possible grandmother. She slowly walked
up to the front desk…why should she be so scared? This woman

probably knew nothing about Rachel Reilly anyway, never mind her extremely confusing lineage, so why was Vera worrying this much? This older woman looked smart and she seemed incredibly kind, so why was Vera afraid of her? Finally Vera made it to the desk...

"Excuse me," Vera said, and the woman looked up at her face and smiled.

"Yes, dear, what can I help you with?"

"Well, this may sound strange, but I was wondering if you knew anything about a woman named Rachel Reilly? I think she may be able to help me with something..."

"Of course I do. She works at Lake Champlain Chocolates and comes in to borrow books all the time. She always brings chocolate to hand out to the children at reading hour. If you wait another ten minutes or so, she should be in to drop off the chocolate for Monday's event," the woman replied with a happy lilt in her voice.

"We can wait. It's really..." but before Vera could get out the word important, a woman with long white hair and bright blue eyes walked through the front door of the library, stopping her words completely. Vera, as if in a trance, approached the woman slowly and deliberately, and held out her hand in greeting before saying, "Hi, my name is Vera Walker. This might sound strange, but you wouldn't happen to be Rachel Reilly, would you?"

The woman's eyes twinkled with what Vera could only describe as a combination of confusion and amusement as she took Vera's hand and, shaking it, replied, "In the flesh. What can I do for you, Vera Walker?"

CHAPTER NINETEEN

V era's eyes widened and Atticus's mouth dropped open.
"You're Rachel Reilly? The descendant of Ella Promur?"

"Guilty, I'm afraid. I see you've been reading about some of your town's folklore," said the woman laughing.

"Yes, I've been doing some research with my best friend and boyfriend, Atticus Wells," Vera said while simultaneously wrapping her arm around him and leaning into his shoulder.

"Atticus? Your parents were kind, and evidently very into literature," Rachel said sarcastically.

"Tell me about it," Atticus responded with a slight laugh.

"So, Miss Vera Walker, what brings you looking for me?"

Vera paused for a few moments and attempted to collect her thoughts; she looked at Atticus who smiled at her. Just his smile gave her strength…but how on earth do you tell a sweet old woman you just met that you think there's a chance that you're her long, lost mind-reading granddaughter? Vera was surprised at the rapidness of her discovery, but she'd only seen eyes that blue on one other person…herself.

"Well," Vera said finally, "It's a long story…"

"I am a frequent visitor to this library, Miss Vera. I love stories, especially long ones. Enlighten me, dear, don't be afraid."

"I'll give you the short version first."

"Very well," Rachel said nodding, though her face held a look of confusion.

"I'm a telepath and I think I'm a descendent of Ella Promur," Vera told Rachel in an unbelievably rushed voice.

"You're a *telepath?*"

"Yes…and I can prove it. Think something. Anything, and I'll tell you what you're thinking."

"Don't be ridiculous, child."

"Please? You have to believe me. I'm telling the truth! "

Something about the way Vera's eyes looked when she asked the questions made Rachel feel like she could trust the girl. Her eyes looked so trusting, so kind, and she hadn't seen eyes so blue since her daughter's.

"Very well. Go on."

Her eyes are so like my Chloe's…they're so blue they're almost mesmerizing. I wonder…

"You wonder what? And who's Chloe?"

"So you *are* a telepath."

Impressive, Rachel added in Vera's head.

Did you just throw a thought at me?

Yes…you seem surprised, yet you can do the same thing…

I just wasn't expecting it…I'm used to being the one throwing the thoughts.

You didn't think you were the only telepath, did you?

Well, until a couple weeks ago, I didn't think telepaths even existed.

You're skeptical, just like Chloe was at first…

Who's Chloe?

Chloe was my daughter.

"Was?" Atticus asked.

"Yes, but, young man, how did you hear that? The gene for telepathy has only ever been found in females, at least in the Promur clan."

"Oh no, no, no...I'm not telepathic or anything. It's just, well, Vera's always been a cautious person...she's been throwing all these thoughts to me. You know, just in case. Can we keep the conversation audible for all parties now? I think Vera might be getting tired."

"I am," Vera said truthfully.

"Very well," Rachel replied, still stunned by the closeness of the teenagers, "I was saying that my daughter Chloe was just as skeptical as you are."

"What happened to Chloe, Mrs. Reilly?" Vera asked cautiously.

"Please, call me Rachel."

"Okay. What happened to Chloe, Rachel?"

"She died in a car crash about sixteen years ago...she and her husband, Matthew Marchmont. Their daughter Ella, named for her ancestor of course, was put up for adoption. I was traveling in Europe at the time of the accident, and I didn't receive word of my daughter's death for quite some time. When I returned to Vermont six months later, Ella was already placed with a family. "

"I'm so sorry," Atticus said, not quite putting all the pieces together. Vera, however, was way ahead of him...her mind racing with her new discoveries.

"My parents died in a car crash when I was just a baby! I don't know anything about them except their first names. My adoptive mother told me my birth mother's name was Chloe and my birth father's name was Matt," and then Vera paused and took a deep breath, "Is it possible that...that *I'm* their daughter?"

Rachel's eyes filled with tears as she walked over to Vera, embracing her, and finally spoke, "As if your telepathy and your story weren't enough...your eyes tell me that without a doubt...you are my Chloe's daughter."

CHAPTER TWENTY

After talking to Rachel for a couple hours in an attempt to try and catch her newly found grandmother up on what her life had been like thus far, and agreeing to begin "telepath" lessons once a week after school, Vera took the bus back to Seckerlyn Center with Atticus. They were late getting home, so they knew that they had to be prepared for a scolding from both households. Atticus called his parents on the way home with the hope that a pre-emptive explanation of the day would smooth things over.

"Hi, Mom? Now before you get all angry I...Mom, please let me talk...I *know* I'm late getting home again, but I have an excellent reason...no, I'm not trying to make excuses...Mom, *seriously* I need to tell you something important!"

Vera swiftly yanked the phone out of Atticus's hand and began talking fast to Mrs. Wells. "Mrs. Wells? Yes, it's Vera...I know we're late but Atticus was telling the truth...no it's not an excuse, I found someone in my family. No, not one of the Walkers. I found a blood relative. Her name is Rachel Reilly...she's my biological mother's mother. Yeah, she's my grandmother. That's why we're late, Mrs.

Wells. We're so, so sorry. Can I take Atticus with me to my house for moral support while I tell my parents? Thank you...love you too. I'll tell him," and Vera hung up the phone.

"Your mom says she loves you," Vera told Atticus matter-of-factly.

"How do you *do* that?"

"Do what?"

"Make her stop yelling."

"It's a gift," Vera said with a grin.

"So," Atticus said changing the topic to one of greater importance, "What are you going to say to them?"

"I don't know, Atticus. What do you say to your parents who raised you for sixteen years? Hey, guess what, Mom and Dad...I found out who my real parents are, and I found an actual blood relative! It's a conversation I thought *they* would be having with *me* at some point. Obviously my feelings weren't worth the trouble."

"I don't think they were thinking along the lines of hurting you, Ver...or keeping you in the dark. They love you...that's why you have to do this. You have to talk to them. I'll be right with you; you'll be fine. I know it."

"Thanks, Finch."

"Anytime, losermuffin," Atticus replied prompting a look from Vera that was an odd mix of amusement, annoyance, and, oddly enough, happiness.

The bus suddenly stopped and let the two of them out. It was a mere ten minute walk to Vera's house from the bus stop which didn't leave Vera much time to think about what she was going to say to her parents. By the time her thoughts stopped racing wildly around in her head, Vera and Atticus were on Vera's front porch. Atticus rang the doorbell and put his arm around Vera.

Mr. Walker answered the door with a stern look on his face. "What kept the two of you?"

Trying to keep her cool, Vera responded quietly, "Dad...I need to talk with you and Mom...and I need Atticus with me."

"Vera, honey, what's wrong?"

"Can we just sit and talk, Dad?" Vera asked impatiently.

"Yeah...sure, honey," Mr. Walker conceded.

Mr. Walker led Vera and Atticus to the living room, and sat next to his wife on the love seat. Vera and Atticus took the couch across from them; Atticus grabbed Vera's hand and gave it a reassuring squeeze.

Mrs. Walker broke the silence, "What's the matter, honey?" she asked wearily with worry.

"Who's Ella Marchmont, Mom and Dad?"

Mr. and Mrs. Walker looked at each other blankly and then back at Vera and Atticus. Mr. Walker spoke first, "Honey, we can explain..."

All of Vera's control seemed to disappear as she started to form words, "Explain? How long have you and Dad known that Vera Walker is synonymous with Ella Marchmont, daughter of Matt and Chloe Marchmont? You have to have known for some time, right? Don't try to lie to me either...I know the two of you had to know something," Vera continued before her parents had time to speak, this time her words were distorted by her tears of sadness, hurt, and anger, "When were you going to tell me anything about my birth parents besides their *first names*? When were you going to tell me I had a *living blood relative* that I could have known for years? How could the two of you keep all of this from me?"

"Vera, you need to calm down. Your father and I were going to tell you on your sixteenth birthday....but you were so upset that day we decided to postpone telling you."

"How long have you known?" she snapped back at her parents.

"Since we adopted you," said Mr. Walker, taking his wife's hand.

"And you sat there and watched me search madly through libraries and the town's historical records for my parents for years? How could you?"

"We were protecting you, Vera," her father said seriously.

"Protecting me from what?"

"From your past."

"From my *past*? So you thought it was better for me to sit idly in the dark and know nothing about my family? What was so scary about my past that I had to be *lied to* for sixteen years?"

"We didn't want people to look at you differently...we knew you were a descendent of Ella Promur...and Promur women have always been, well, *different*."

Trying to gage how much her parents knew about the Promur family line, Vera asked, "Different how?"

"Promur women," her father began, "have always been rumored to have certain abilities of the mind...I guess you could call them 'telepaths' for lack of a better word. In town folklore, descendants of Ella Promur are described as mind-readers. We were skeptical, but, none the less, we couldn't take any risks with your safety. If you were to develop such gifts, we wanted you to be able to use them when necessary, but not be burdened by them. We didn't want to you become a spectacle. We didn't want people asking questions."

"Well, guess what, Mom and Dad, I'm a spectacle," Vera said flatly.

"Vera," her mother asked cautiously, "Are you saying you inherited the abilities of your ancestors?"

"Yep, I'm a full blown freak, and thanks to the two of you, I had no warning whatsoever," Vera said coldly.

"You're not a freak, Vera," Atticus said with conviction.

"The sympathy is nice, Atticus, but is now really the time?" Vera snapped before considering her words. After seeing the look on Atticus's face Vera's eyes began to glisten with tears she was desperately trying to hold in.

"I'm sorry, Atticus."

"You don't need to apologize," he said removing his hand from hers and proceeding to use it to rub Vera's back gently.

"How many people know about your powers, Vera?" her father asked seriously.

"Just Atticus, the two of you, and Rachel Reilly, my long-lost grandmother that you never told me about."

"Vera Eleanor Walker, you need to stop your yelling this minute," Mrs. Walker demanded.

"I'm not yelling...I'm speaking sternly," Vera said with sarcasm.

"Your father and I are *so* sorry we didn't tell you sooner. We thought we were doing what was best for you...thought we were keeping you safe."

"Keeping me safe? How did this keep me safe? It's not like telling me the truth would have done any harm. Keeping it from the public is one thing...but you *lied* to *me*. It's not like I was going to walk around school going, 'Hi, I'm Vera and I can read minds.' School is hard enough to survive without adding in a 'freak factor.'"

"Vera, remember what we talked about. These are your parents...they love you. They wouldn't hurt you on purpose," Atticus said grabbing Vera's hand again. Then turning to Mr. and Mrs. Walker he added, "That being said, how could the two of you keep this from her? Vera deserved to know the truth. She's kind and trustworthy and loyal. *You* should have trusted her. I think you know that."

Both of the Walkers stared at Atticus for an unnerving few seconds before finding their voices, "Yes. We know that," Mr. Walker said not looking Atticus in the eye.

"We're so sorry, Vera," her mother added.

Vera, finally calming down, took a deep breath, smiled at Atticus through her subsiding tears, and then faced her parents, "I know and I'm sorry for yelling...but you've got to know how hard this has been for me. I've felt so lost and so scared and I had no answers. I didn't even have a hunch. Now all the answers just came through the floodgates and it's like my brain is in overload."

Mr. and Mrs. Walker walked towards the couch and sat near Vera. Vera looked at the two of them, searching their eyes for answers she knew may never appear, and then, without tears, she hugged both of them. "I love you both, Mom and Dad...I just wish I had known."

"In hindsight, we wish you had known too," Mr. Walker said.

CHAPTER TWENTY-ONE

B y the time Monday rolled along, everyone in school had found out about Vera and Atticus dating: one of the disadvantages to living in an unbelievably small town. When the two walked into school hand-in-hand the entire student body was in a buzz. Ashliana, Evan, Kyle, and Chelsea had practically pounced on the two them demanding to know how and when they became a couple. The two had promised to disclose all details to their interested and joyous friends at the end of the day over a pizza downtown.

Vera was suddenly aware of how grateful she was that she had learned to control her mind-reading before she and Atticus started dating, but her relief was stifled by her desire to see Rachel again. Walking the halls of Arcadia High School listening to her classmates talk about her and Atticus dating seemed trivial compared to the knowledge she had gained over the weekend...

She came from a family of telepaths. She had a grandmother who she had never met until two days ago. Her parents knew she could read minds, and they were oddly cool with it. Vera could hardly keep focused on school with all this news, never mind the never ending dull, humdrum student body conversations.

Vera had to admit, of course, that there were perks to being a couple where one of the two could both read minds and throw thoughts; Vera and Atticus slowly discovered this over the first couple weeks of their relationship. It was incredibly easy to have private conversations, just like the one they had in the library, in class, without anyone being aware. They could tell each other private jokes without anyone else being confused or feeling left out. They could plan out their afternoons and help each other with schoolwork without having to be annoying and talk in class.

Vera also was able to talk to Atticus about Rachel, who she had begun visiting three times a week, rather than just her agreed one time a week, for the obvious reasons of getting to know her, as well as for training in her telepathic abilities. According to Rachel, Vera hadn't even begun to tap into her most powerful and dangerous gifts, and Rachel was determined to help Vera use and control them so that she would be a danger neither to herself nor anyone around her. Besides her mind-reading and thought-throwing, Vera was told that she would eventually be powerful enough to control someone's mind; this didn't appeal to Vera in the least as the idea of controlling her own mind and someone else's seemed almost immoral. Rachel, however, told Vera that there may come times when it might be a useful gift to have.

While in school, Vera and Atticus found mind-talking during Miss Barnes's English class to be the most enjoyable. For Atticus, it gave him something to keep his mind off of Miss Barnes constantly making literary references out of his name, and for Vera, who had read *To Kill a Mockingbird* at least five times, it gave her a chance to help Atticus with the book without looking overly conspicuous…she also often used the time to fill Atticus in on any and all information pertaining to her private "telepathy" lessons. Atticus never tired of hearing about Vera's new skills; being a fan of the supernatural and of magic, Atticus thought Vera's new abilities were about the coolest things he had ever encountered.

Come the beginning of third week of their relationship, the English class was still reading *To Kill a Mockingbird*; Vera was delighted as usual and Atticus was less than thrilled. Miss Barnes began writing important characters, plots, themes, and quotes on the board for the class to discuss. Vera seized the free moment and tried to start up a mental conversation with Atticus...

Atticus? Atticus? Finch?!?

> *For God's sake...what, Vera?*

Just saying hi...are you enjoying our class today? Note the sarcasm...

> *Very funny, Ver...and for the record, you don't need to add the "note the sarcasm" because **I can hear you**, remember? But anyways...you know full well this is less than my favorite class of the day...and you do realize what we're reading, right?*

Yeah...hence the humor in the situation.

> *Haha, your hilarity astounds me, Ver, it really does. But seriously, we've been reading this book forever...*

Oh come on, you big losermuffin. Think on the bright side...just get through this week and then on Friday you will have your undoubtedly awesome sixteenth birthday party complete with cake, ice cream, presents, family, friends, and, of course, your wonderful best friend turned girlfriend: me.

> *I know, Ver...but seriously does she have to look at me every time she says the name "Atticus?" It's slightly ridiculous. Plus, she always gives me the "I love you eyes" when she looks at me....like I'm the character. It's sickening. Distract me...tell me more about your powers and Rachel...*

Don't be such a baby, Atticus. The class is almost over...

> *...have to get those papers...without them my career is ruined, I'll be nothing...I need to publish those student papers...*

Atticus, did you hear that?

Ver, let's review: you're the one with the powers not me. So, if you just heard a thought, then I didn't hear it too. The only thoughts I hear are the ones you send to me.

Atticus, I need to talk you after class. The bell's going to ring any second now.

Ver, what the hell is wrong?

I told you, I'll tell you in a second.

The bell rang immediately after Atticus heard Vera's last words. Vera quickly grabbed Atticus's hand and pulled him out of his chair with so much force it surprised him.

"Ver, will you please tell me what's wrong? You're freaking me out."

"I heard Principal McCormac's thoughts. He must have walked right behind you when I was focusing on your thoughts."

"You're sure they were his thoughts?" Atticus asked perplexed.

"Yes. Finch, I recognized his voice," Vera said in a voice that hinted at annoyance, "He passed by our classroom right before the bell."

"Right. So what's so troubling about what you heard?"

"Well he was thinking something along the lines of being ruined if he didn't get some student papers published."

"And that's a big deal because...?"

"Because, based on what I heard, it sounds like he's stealing student papers and using them to better his career," Vera said to her friend as if she had made an unbelievable discovery.

"Wow...harsh. I'm sorry, Vera, but that's just plain ridiculous. He could need the papers to publish in a student magazine...or to send to colleges. Why are you assuming the worst? I think you should just let it go, Ver. You're probably just jumping to conclusions. I'm sure if Rachel were here she would tell you the same thing."

"Leave Rachel out of this, Atticus. It's not ridiculous and I'm not jumping to conclusions. It makes perfect sense. He's always been pompous and arrogant....you and I have *never* liked him. Plus, how many essays has he published? Why is it so unbelievable to think that some of 'his essays' were actually written by students? The pieces fit, Atticus! Why won't you just trust me on this?"

After angrily stating her point to Atticus, Vera searched his head to get an idea of where his mind was at.

Of course I trust her, but...

"But what, Atticus?"

"But I...wait a second," Atticus said quietly out of anyone else's earshot but Vera's, looking suddenly angry and hurt, "Did you just read my mind, Vera?"

"I, well...," Vera stuttered nervously.

"You did!" Atticus said, his voice level rising, "Vera, you promised you wouldn't use that against me! I thought you trusted me enough to tell you the truth, just like I trust you to tell me the truth. Just like we always *trust each other*. Hell, Vera, *Rachel* trusts me and she just met me...she knows that I would never betray you, never hurt you... I didn't know you thought so little of me that you would actually go as far as to spy on me when I was ready and willing to tell you the truth!"

"Well, it's not like you trust *me*, Atticus—"

"I did," Atticus said upset and matter-of-factly, cutting her off and then turning to walk away.

"What do you mean you *did*?" Vera questioned.

"I think my meaning is clear enough," said Atticus over his shoulder as he continued to walk away.

"Fine, walk away, Atticus. Be a coward. Maybe this whole relationship thing was a stupid idea after all," Vera said, intentionally trying to hurt Atticus for the first time ever.

Atticus stopped dead in his tracks, paused, and then said, "You know what, Ver? I don't just *think* it was a stupid idea, I *know* it was a stupid idea because you know what? All this time through everything we've been through, I've never doubted you. I've never strayed, never betrayed you, I've never made you feel anything but special. But even you're fallible, Vera…just like I am. Believe it or not, even you have weaknesses. Your powers don't make you perfect and they don't make you superhuman. The sad thing is, I think I know you, the good and the bad, better than you do and that's a real shame."

"Atticus, I…"

"No, Vera, let me finish," Atticus said putting his hand up to interrupt her and staring intently into her eyes, "I know that you keep a journal, full of only quotes, and that you read it when you need inspiration or guidance. I know that when you're scared you, without knowing it, fold and unfold your hands over and over again to try to calm down. I know you never mention your birth family in front of your mom, dad, and brothers because you don't want to hurt their feelings. I know that your favorite movie is *The Sound of Music*, because you see strength in Maria that you desperately want to see you yourself. I know that you'd rather dip apples in chocolate than in caramel, because you think caramel feels funny in your mouth. I know that you secretly want a tattoo even though you're terrified of needles. But I was a fool because, obviously, even though I know all that…I never knew…never thought…never *fathomed* that you would think I was a thoughtless coward. I guess I don't know so much after all. In fact, I don't think I know you at all, Vera. And you sure as hell don't know me or trust me."

And slowly, Atticus turned and began to walk away from Vera, who called after him in a voice full of unintentional desperation, "Atticus, wait…"

"Why?" Atticus said turning quickly to glare at her.

Vera opened her mouth and closed it again unable to speak, tears welling up in her eyes.

"That's what I thought…wish you could have proven my fears wrong. It's ironic that the one time you actually manage to keep your mouth shut is the one time your words could have saved this relationship, but you can't even bring yourself to say one thing. I feel truly sorry for you, Vera Walker. I wish I was worth fighting for," Atticus said defeated and walked away leaving her standing alone in the hallway, agape, in tears, and speechless until the words she had been holding in slipped out as a mixture between a whisper and a stifled sob.

"You are worth fighting for, Atticus Wells."

CHAPTER TWENTY-TWO

"Atticus called again today, Vera. I think it would be in your best interest to talk to him," Rachel Reilly said to her granddaughter who looked about as ready for a telepathy lesson as literature's Tom Sawyer was to white-wash a fence. Vera looked down-trodden and simply dismal and she wasn't accomplishing any amount of learning whatsoever. Teaching Vera in this state, Rachel thought, was equivalent to trying to teach tricks to a pet rock.

"Did you hear me, dear? Vera?" Rachel asked, trying again to get Vera's attention.

"Yes, and as you know, I disagree," Vera said rushed and impolitely.

"What could he have done that has made you this upset with him?" Rachel asked ardently, "He has never left your side…never betrayed you."

"It's not what he *did*, Rachel, it's what he didn't do. He didn't… he *doesn't* trust me," Vera said while looking down and twirling the ring on her finger round and round out of nervousness.

"You're spinning the ring on your finger," Rachel said casually with a small almost imperceptible smile.

"Yes. And?" Vera asked rudely, eyebrows raised suspiciously.

"And," Rachel answered in a calm, reminiscent tone, "Chloe used to do that...usually when she was upset or when she felt guilty about something. It seems you have a lot of your mother in you. You wouldn't happen to be taking the anger you have for your own actions out on Atticus, now would you?"

"Rachel, I am not mad at *myself*...I am mad at *Atticus*. He's the one that messed everything up. He ruined everything...he's the one that decided I wasn't a good enough friend to earn his *precious trust*."

"Well, you certainly proved his doubts right then when you read his mind without permission...something that you promised him you wouldn't do," Rachel said coolly.

"Whose side are you on anyways? I'm your granddaughter... you're supposed to be telling me that I'm right and that I deserve an apology!" Vera said in a whiny, discontented voice.

"First of all, there are no sides in this argument. Also, as your grandmother I have no obligation to tell you you're right all the time or to pity you when you don't deserve pity. It is my obligation, however, to mold you into the best person you can be..."

"I am being the best I can be, Rachel! I deserve to be angry...I deserve to have feelings," Vera said through an overabundance of angry tears.

"You are entitled to feel however you want. But you should know that you and Atticus are both angry and, pardon my saying this, but you, my dear, are blowing things way out of proportion." Vera opened her mouth to talk but Rachel put her hand up as if to silence her just as Atticus had. Vera's mouth closed almost immediately, much to her own dismay. Rachel then continued.

"Atticus cares about you, he probably even loves you, and you think he doesn't trust you? He knows, like I've come to know very quickly, that you are the queen of jumping to unnecessary conclusions and Atticus wanted to talk some sense into you before one of the aforesaid conclusions got you into trouble. Is that so wrong? Wanting to protect you, he lost you. He has called me every night this week asking me to ask you to call him. He has called your house, he has knocked on your door, and what have you done? You decided to hide and pout and I think you know that there is no glory in that. Let me tell you, I have seen my fair share of teenage boys...you have the friendship and love of a truly good one. Atticus is one in a million, and that's saying something. If you throw that friendship and love away over your foolish pride, then you are not the girl I thought you were...and you are certainly not a PROMUR."

"Are you finished?"

"Not yet...a few more words and then you may take your leave if you must. Vera, if you remember nothing else I say today remember this: you must live up to your name...live up to the standards of the beauty that's concealed inside you. The name Vera means truth... you are blessed with the ability to hear the inner-most truths in the minds of others, and that's certainly amazing, but until you embrace the truths hiding deep within yourself you will never be whole, never get a chance to recognize the beautiful truths that are inside of you. Don't let your pride separate your truths from your beauty, because then you will be witness to the tragedy of seeing only the ugly truths in your life, and that, my lovely Vera, would be truly heartbreaking. Because the ugly part of the truth...it's a façade created by a trickster inside of you. Don't let your inner demons consume you, Vera, but rather let yourself be consumed by unseen miracles; let yourself be consumed by beautiful truth."

Vera stared at Rachel for a few moments opening and closing her mouth. Never before had Vera been silenced; never before had Vera been rendered speechless. She stared into her grandmother's exquisite blue eyes and for the first time, those eyes–so much like her own—seemed to frighten her, not because they were threatening, but because it seemed to Vera that they were seeing her for the first time. Vera quickly turned away and walked towards the door.

"Goodbye, Rachel. I can't be here...I have to go...I have to go right now."

"I can see you, Vera, and Atticus can see you. Please, never be afraid to see yourself."

Vera opened the door, and without turning replied, "I'm not afraid," and then walked out slamming the door behind her.

"Yes, yes you are," Rachel said to the air that just moments ago had held her granddaughter.

CHAPTER TWENTY-THREE

Atticus had never been more relieved for a Friday to come in his entire life. First, because Friday was his birthday, and practically the entire school would be coming to his house for a sixteenth birthday pool party and cookout, and second, because he could better avoid eye daggers from his ex-girlfriend. Ex-friend too, apparently, as Vera hadn't graced Atticus with a single word all week even after their friends had tried to talk to her…

The day after the two of them fought, Atticus had walked to Vera's house in an attempt to smooth things over and offer to walk her to school. Needless to say, it was a futile attempt as Vera had decided to walk to school with Ashliana, who, too, became Vera's verbal punching bag on the way to school after she insisted Vera grace Atticus with a few words. When Atticus got to English and sat next to Vera in his usual seat, Vera promptly got up and found a seat on the other side of the classroom. Later that day, Atticus called Rachel (using the phone number she had given him for emergencies) asking to talk to Vera. Even though Rachel seemed to think it was a good idea, Vera refused to talk to him. After that,

Atticus gave up trying to get her attention in school (though he did try to call her several other times)...as did the rest of their mutual friends, all of whom Vera was ignoring.

━≺┤ ├≻━

Vera's parents told her that Atticus had stopped by to walk her to school, but Vera's fiery temper and extraordinary grudge holding abilities made it impossible for her to approach Atticus and talk with him. Instead, she decided to constantly shoot dirty looks in his direction and give him the silent treatment for a week. Granted, she knew these actions were stupid and childish, but Vera was angry; she allowed her anger to drive her rather than her good sense.

━≺┤ ├≻━

Invitations to Atticus's birthday bash had been placed in the lockers of all who were desired to attend on the Wednesday of that week. Atticus had struggled all week with the dilemma of whether or not to invite his "ice queen" of a best friend. In the end he decided that Vera had to come to his party...she had gone to all of his parties since he was old enough to enjoy them. It would be foolhardy and immature to neglect to give her an invitation.

━≺┤ ├≻━

Vera was surprised to get Atticus's invitation, and contemplated whether or not she would go. She began to think of all the excuses she could use: short notice, stomach bug, had to watch her brothers...none of the excuses seemed good enough to her. Angry or not, Vera still considered Atticus her closest friend and she knew it would hurt him a lot if she didn't show up to his party. By the time

111

Friday rolled around, Vera had decided to "make an appearance" at Atticus's party out of politeness (plus she didn't want to upset Mr. and Mrs. Wells).

After what seemed to be the longest English class ever, complete with several *To Kill a Mockingbird* references coupled with what was now becoming routine silence from Vera, Atticus jumped up from his chair as the bell rang and ran out the door to get ready for his party that night.

Vera watched her friend longingly, a big part of her wanting to say something to him...anything to him...just a simple "Happy Birthday" or "hello..." But once again, her pride got in the way, and Vera walked to her locker alone. It looked like her weekend was shaping up to be just as dismal as her past week at school... all because of her foolishness. Even with her ongoing telepathy lessons, Vera's week had been terrible. Without Atticus to talk to, she had no outlet for all her new information...the one person that truly understood her was "out of bounds". She had contemplated telling Ashliana and Chelsea but it seemed too risky; plus she'd taken to ignoring them too as they constantly begged her to speak to Atticus and she had become increasingly bitter and annoyed. No, she couldn't burden her friends, especially after paying no attention to them for a solid week, and *she* had made the decision to put Atticus on hold...a decision she was "just going to have to live with and deal with" Rachel had told her. The trouble was, Vera wished she didn't have to deal with it. She just wanted things to go back to normal...well, as normal as possible. She had to fix things, but she didn't know how to forgive her own conceit and stupidity in order to do so. And if she couldn't forgive herself, how in the world were her friends going to forgive her?

CHAPTER TWENTY-FOUR

By the time Vera plucked up enough courage to go to Atticus's house for his party the rest of the guests had already been there for over an hour. Vera walked over to Mr. and Mrs. Wells and put her gift for Atticus on the table.

Atticus's parents smiled widely upon seeing Vera. Mrs. Wells spoke first, "Vera, honey, we've missed you this week! We're sorry you and Atticus aren't getting along; we miss seeing you, and we know Atticus misses you too. In fact, he was just telling me and Dean the other night that without you he feels—"

A stern, yet polite voice cut her off, "Not now, Mom, please."

Atticus stood directly behind Vera his face looking more concerned and embarrassed than assertive.

Mrs. Wells seemed to backtrack, realizing her mistake in embarrassing her son, "Of course, Atticus, I didn't realize—"

"It's no big deal, Mom," Atticus said, and then added courteously, "Thanks for the party, by the way. It's great."

"Of course," Mr. Wells said without hesitation, "You're a good kid, Atticus. You make us proud. You deserve this…your Mom and I are going to go and get the cake. We'll let you and Vera catch up."

"Thanks, Dad," Atticus said and then turned and looked at Vera.

Vera swallowed hard out of nervousness and guilt. After a few seconds of awkward silence between the two of them, Vera spoke in a timid and fragile voice.

"Hi, Finch."

"Wow, so that's what it feels like to exist…I had forgotten. I'm happy to see, or hear, rather, that you still have full use of your vocal chords."

"Please, don't do that, Atticus."

"Do what, Vera? Comment on the fact that I might as well have been invisible to you this entire week or how you didn't even have the decency to wish me a simple 'Happy Birthday' in school today? Need I mention the fact that you've also been a total jerk to all of our friends this week?"

"I already feel bad enough, okay? And I came to your party, didn't I? I almost didn't come because I'm so embarrassed and ashamed. But I did come…I didn't completely blow you off."

"No, Vera, you're right…you did come to my party. But you didn't come for me. You came because you felt *obligated*. You felt *guilty*. Ten bucks says my feelings had close to nothing to do with your decision."

"Atticus…" Vera began in a somber yet urgent tone before being completely ignored.

"Twenty bucks says you came to talk to me because you feel trapped in your own skin and need to use me as a person to vent to. And thirty bucks says you contemplated telling other people about your issues, but then chickened out and decided I was your only option."

"Nice, Atticus. I come to your party to try and show you that I forgive you for what you did to me, and all you do is start accusing—"

Atticus cut Vera off quickly. His eyes flared with rage and irritation.

"Are you serious, Vera? *You* forgive *me?* When *you* were the one that started the whole fight in the first place? The one who accused our outwardly arrogant, but innocent, principal of publishing student work as his own? The one who constantly jumps to conclusions that, quite frankly, make no sense whatsoever? The one who betrayed my trust, invaded my privacy, and then ignored me for a week even after I tried to come to your house and work things out? After I called Rachel, your newly found grandmother and a woman I hardly know, to try and get you to speak to me? After I went so far as to beg Ash to talk to you for me because nothing else was working? *You* forgive *me?*"

"Principal McCormac is stealing those papers and I'm going to prove it, Atticus! I don't care if you don't believe me. I don't need you anyway. I have Rachel now…you're just a mistrusting jerk who thinks it's more important to think logically than trust his best friend."

"Wait, I can trust you now? Because the last time I did it didn't turn out so well for me. And the last time I checked you'd rather see me as a literal 'invisible man' than a best friend. Unless best friends ignore and betray each other; if that's the case then you, Vera Eleanor Walker, are the *best friend I've ever had*…you should be *really proud*," Atticus said, his voicing dripping with sarcasm and full of anger.

"That's right, Atticus, keep up the guilt trips."

"Guilt trips? Vera, I'm not giving you a guilt trip, I'm telling you the truth. Something you clearly don't understand."

"You want the truth, Atticus? I *hate you*. Happy now?"

"Blissfully…that may have been the first honest thing you've said to me all day. Bravo, Vera. *Bravo.*"

As he spoke, Vera turned on the spot and began to walk away quickly and deliberately; Atticus called after her.

"Where are you going now?"

"What do you care?"

"I'm curious…plus it's kind of rude to leave a party before the cake. Then again…rude and you fit pretty well together right now, so never mind."

"Not that it's any of your business, but I'm going to the school to prove to you that I'm right about Principal McCormac."

"Vera, don't be an idiot."

"You don't have to watch out for me, Atticus. I don't need you anymore, remember? Stay at your stupid party. I can take care of myself."

"Fine, Vera, be a horrible, self-centered little princess. See if I care."

"I *know* you don't care, you arrogant prick!"

"Nice, Ver…breaking out the big guns because of a lack of vocabulary?" Atticus asked, his voice oozing mockery.

"That means a lot coming from a person who reads…oh wait… do you read at all, Atticus?"

"Just leave, Vera, and don't talk to me…after hearing your voice again I'm thinking your silence was preferable."

"Go to hell."

"Right back at you, you spoiled brat. Happy Birthday to me! Way to kill the birthday buzz, ice queen."

And the two of them turned back to back and walked purposefully in opposite directions.

CHAPTER TWENTY-FIVE

V era walked into the darkened school through the front door. With any luck, she would be able to confront Principal McCormac about what she heard and be out of the school in no time; the school hallways were creepy without any overhead lights on, and Vera felt uncomfortable walking in them alone. As she walked, it felt to Vera that the walls were watching her and tracking her every move...

It was a good thing that Vera could walk the halls of her high school in her sleep, because as she got closer to Principal McCormac's office there seemed to be less and less light aiding her on her way; she could have sworn she could feel her pupils dilating as she walked the halls. Whether this was caused by her strange fear or because of the lack of light, she was unsure. Vera slowly approached the office; through the glass door Principal McCormac was still sitting at his desk hunched over a stack of papers. From a distance, he looked worried and exhausted.

Vera was just about to knock on his door when she spotted something interesting on the bulletin board next to his office. The following words marked the top of the bulletin board:

SELECT STUDENT ESSAYS CHOSEN TO BE
SUBMITTED TO PRESTIGIOUS NATIONAL ESSAY
CONTEST
*WINNERS CHOSEN BY MISS BARNES AND PRINCIPAL
MCCORMAC*

Below the title were several papers, her own included, tacked onto the board on display for students and faculty to look at and read through. Slowly but surely Vera began to have an epiphany: Principal McCormac wasn't stealing papers; he was reading them to give to a National Contest Committee. Atticus didn't cause the fight between the two of them. She had. Of course she knew this already, but it hurt more to have it come flying at her face without warning. Atticus hadn't doubted her intellect…he had thought clearly. Atticus had been there for her through thick and thin, never failing to help her. She let him down, insulted him, *betrayed him.*

"Oh God, what have I done? Why did I push him away?" Vera said quietly to herself.

"I was about to ask you where your annoying knight in shining armor was, but it seems that might be unnecessary," an eerily familiar voice said behind Vera.

Vera turned around slowly, only to find herself face-to-face with Charles Jenkins. She gasped and backed into the wall behind her, using its solidity to remain in balance.

"Aww…did you miss me, Vera?"

"Charles," Vera said fearfully, "What are you doing here?"

"Oh, no one told you? It's May, Vera. My school let me out a week ago. Ironic, isn't it, that us messed up kids get to get out of school before all of you adorable public school kids?"

"Not all students at your school are messed up, Charles. In fact most are pretty amazing individuals from what I hear...you seem to be the exception," said Vera trying to remain calm and in control.

"Ah, I see you did your research on my lovely military institution...you just obviously overlooked our academic calendar. You are right though, Vera, those military kids are too structured, too polite for me. I do feel like the odd man out," Charles added with a tone of sarcastic sadness.

"I hope you don't expect me to pity you."

"There's my Vera. The witty spit-fire."

"Trust me, *I'm not your Vera.*"

"Oh, I think you are. At least you will be...soon."

"I'm not afraid of you. Principal McCormac is right in his office. One scream from me and he'll know something's wrong. He'll come and help me."

"Oh...poor, innocent, naïve Vera Walker. Did you really think that I would take a chance like that? I tranquilized the poor sucker right after I realized you were coming here to see him. It wasn't hard to beat you to the school...you have very short legs."

"You followed me here?"

"Vera, I've been trailing you for weeks now, whenever I could escape from school grounds, and you didn't even know it."

"The man in green my brothers recognized in the woods! That *was* you!" Vera said horrified at her discovery.

"Bingo, we have a winner! You do catch on fast, Vera."

"Why would you try to hurt them?!?! They're only eleven!"

"Oh, Vera, can't you see? I didn't want anything to do with them. They were collateral if anything. I lured them into the woods to try and get you," Charles said with a sadistic smile, "Unfortunately, as usual, your stupid buffoon of a best friend was with you and I really didn't feel like getting in another fist fight. Lucky you. You got away scotch free."

"Why are you doing this?" Vera asked pleadingly.

"Because, Vera, I want you. Can't you see that? You deserve a guy like me. A guy that's strong and handsome. You just don't know it yet. So I came here to help you to see reason," Charles said too calmly. "And if you don't see to reason, well, I'll have to defer to my tranquilizers…or my handgun. It's usually pretty effective."

Charles pulled out a small handgun and pointed it at Vera. Vera's mind began to race with options. Trying to send a mind-message to Atticus was out of the question: she couldn't penetrate the walls and reach the distance to Atticus's house with her thoughts, and with the way she had been treating him, she wouldn't have been surprised if he didn't come at all even if she did call. Regardless, Rachel hadn't trained her to that level of her power yet. She could run, but Charles would surely catch up with her. She could try to "play along with Charles" and then make a break for it at an appropriate time, but in all honestly she knew she couldn't lie that well.

Vera's leg hit the trash can in front of the principal's office. Instinctively and out of the impulse to escape via any means necessary, Vera grabbed the trash can and threw it at Charles, who yelled in pain as the metal can hit his face, and then broke into a sprint down the deserted, dark hallway.

Vera raced through the darkened corridors of the school, constantly looking over her shoulder, hoping to lose the person rapidly pursuing her. She could still hear him behind her—his heavy breathing and his angry screams. In desperation, Vera called out to Atticus, hoping he would come to help her even though she knew he was too far away to hear her. Why did she say she didn't need him? She needed Atticus; he was everything to her…how could she just push him away?

Seeing no other way out, Vera ran for the art room; she couldn't outrun him forever, but maybe she could hide long enough to plan an escape and go to the police. Vera spotted the tall art cabinet in the corner of the room; it wasn't the best hiding place, but it was all she could think of with the time she had. As soon as she settled herself into the cabinet, she could hear heavy footsteps approach the door.

Vera held her breath and cupped her hands over her mouth, fingernails digging into her cheeks. The footsteps were in the room now, and they were coming towards her hiding place. Vera began to cry silently. If he found her, he would surely kill her... she knew too much... and then she would never be able to see her family and friends again. She would never get the chance to tell Atticus how much he meant to her.

Suddenly the breathing became louder and the footsteps stopped...right in front of the cabinet. Vera braced herself as the cabinet doors were forced open. She sat speechless as the shadow in front of her said, "Vera Walker, did you really think I wouldn't find you?"

CHAPTER TWENTY-SIX

"Atticus?" Vera asked surprised, looking up at him through a sea of tears.

"Yeah, Ver, you losermuffin, it's me. We've got to get you out of here. Charles is headed towards the locker rooms so we don't have much time before he doubles back."

"You called me losermuffin..."

"Well, it's certainly fitting for you this week, and not in a facetious way either. You really have been a huge losermuffin this week. All that aside, *you* need to be quiet right now so *we* can get out of here before Norman Bates comes back and—"

"Why did you come? How did you find me?" Vera asked, interrupting Atticus's thought process.

"Seriously, Vera, can we talk about this later? I think our main concern should be getting you out of the building...getting you someplace safe."

"Tell me," Vera said adamantly, her tears subsiding.

"I came because I wanted to be sure you were safe. You left in a hurry and then I had a bad feeling so I came, okay?"

"But…"

"Ver, now is *really* not the time to become even more loquacious than usual, trust me. Can we go now?"

"Finch, since when do you use words like…"

"Ver, we don't have time to argue. You can fight with me later. I promise."

Vera looked up at him disappointed and replied, "Fine."

Atticus grabbed Vera's hand, a gesture that she didn't even try to resist as it made Vera feel safe, and led her slowly, but calculatingly down the hallway, back towards Principal McCormac's office. The front door was almost in sight…just a few hallways to go. All he had to do was get her out and call 911. Nothing else mattered at the moment.

Vera, finally realizing how much of a risk her friend had taken coming to rescue her, squeezed Atticus's hand and whispered, "Atticus? I messed up…I jumped to conclusions. I hurt you," slowly her tears were bubbling up again, "I'm, I'm so sorry."

"That doesn't matter now, Ver. What matters is that—"

Atticus's words were interrupted by a gun shot that missed Atticus by inches and shattered the glass entry to the principal's office. Mechanically and without thought, Atticus turned around and tucked Vera behind his back, using his body as a shield.

"Aww, this is adorable. Atticus Wells, the stereotypical hero, comes rushing to the rescue of his fair maiden. How truly touching. You know, Atticus, this didn't work out so well for your literary counterpart….didn't Tom Robinson, the colored man Atticus defends in the book, die at the end?"

"I'm not defending Tom Robinson from a bigoted jury in court now am I, Charles? Believe it or not, besides my name, the book and my life share very few similarities."

"I suppose, Atticus, I suppose. But I can see parallels in both plots. For one, in the book someone dies and I hate to tell you, but here someone's going to die too."

Behind Atticus, Vera began to sob.

"Oh, don't cry, Vera," Charles said with false reassurance while walking closer to both Vera and Atticus, "You won't be the one dying...Atticus here will be," he added throwing a hard punch into Atticus's stomach causing him to double over in pain, but, determined, he amazingly held his ground between Charles and Vera.

Charles continued, "It'll be much more tragic, don't you think? No fairytale crap in this story. This is real life! The good guy doesn't win. Plus, Vera, didn't you say you didn't need your white knight anymore?"

Vera wrapped her arm around Atticus's chest as if to try and protect him, "No, please don't, Charles. Don't hurt him!"

"So you *do* have feelings for this *scum*, don't you Vera?" Charles yelled while backhanding Atticus with his handgun, laughing as his victim fell to floor and then began to struggle to get back in front of Vera, blood dripping down his forehead, " Oh well, too little too late I say," and he pointed the gun at Atticus's chest just as he was regaining his balance.

Vera didn't know what compelled her to move, but before she consciously knew what she was doing, she had walked in front of Atticus and stood statue-like in front of him.

"No, Ver, don't," Atticus said with strength though his voice gave his pain away.

"If you're going to shoot Atticus, you'll have to shoot me first."

"Vera, no," Atticus said pleadingly behind her trying to pull her back. Vera, however, remained planted firmly in front of him.

"How cliché of you, Vera. You even used the stupid corny line... sorry to disappoint though, Vera, that line only works on shows like 'The OC' and 'One Tree Hill'. Too bad for you."

"I'm serious, Charles. You'll have to shoot me before you can even hope to get to Atticus…"

"Vera, you don't have to do this," Atticus said still clutching his bleeding head, but obviously gaining strength.

"Atticus...trust me. *Please*," Vera replied, her blue eyes piercing into him giving him a strange hope and security, "He won't shoot me," she added, turning back to Charles.

"You'd never shoot *me* would you, Charles?"

You need me. You want me, right?...

"Wait, how did you..." Charles said looking confused.

"I'm no use to you dead. After all, what fun could I possibly be dead? All limp and unresponsive," Vera said, her tone gaining a certain strangeness with every word.

"Get out of the way, Vera," Charles said, the confidence in his voice changing to fear.

Vera continued to walk closer and closer to Charles who had slowly begun to back up, "No. I don't think I will."

"I said," Charles said, trying to sound menacing, "Get out of my way, Vera."

"No."

You're so dense, Charles. How can you even stand yourself?

"What? Stop messing with me! Move over!"

"I told you...you'll have to shoot me," Vera said giving Charles the most evil and cryptic look she could conjure.

And you won't do it. You're a coward, Charles Jenkins, you won't do it.

"What the hell?!?! How are you doing that?"

"Doing what, Charles? I'm only walking towards you."

You're a pathetic excuse for a person. You're scum. And you know it... don't you?

"Stop it, Vera!"

"What's the matter, Charles?"

Hearing voices?

Vera was just a foot away from him now. Her eyes bore into him like venom.

"Vera, stop," Charles said, losing control.

"Stop what, Charles?"

You worthless piece of shit.

"Leave me alone! Stop it!"

Did you really think you could come back and win me over? I could NEVER like someone as repulsive as you. What are you compared to Atticus? You're nothing but an arrogant, cowardly snake.

Vera moved the gun so that it pointed away from her chest. She pushed Charles up against the wall.

"What's got you spooked, Charles? I'm not **that** intimidating…"

Am I?

"Stop it!"

"You're weak…"

I knew you'd never shoot me.

"Just stop, I'll do whatever you want!"

*Anything I want….wow, you're pathetic. You're **nothing**.*

Out of nowhere, Atticus suddenly heard Vera's voice…

Once I move, grab the gun.

Quickly she moved her thoughts back to Charles.

Who would ever want anything from you?

"Get out of my head!"

"I only want one thing…"

One simple thing…

"Leave me alone!"

Revenge. You sick-minded bastard.

And Vera punched Charles square in the jaw and then shoved his shooting hand against the wall causing him to cringe in pain and, in the confusion, drop the gun. Atticus ran, grabbing the gun just as Vera had told him to, but Charles had recovered.

"Vera, look out!" Atticus yelled to his friend, but Charles was quick, and he threw Vera against the wall, and she fell down, seemingly unconscious.

Atticus ran to his injured friend only to have Charles lunge at him in an attempt to grab the gun. The two fought on the floor until Charles over-powered the already injured Atticus, punching him in the nose and stealing the gun from his grasp.

Charles stood over Atticus with the gun pointed towards his head, his teeth red and forming a satanic, bloody smile, "Did you really think you could outsmart me? You, the guy who Vera admitted she doesn't have any use for? The guy she doesn't need? You're no hero, Atticus Wells, you're a joke. Say goodbye... you *worthless piece of crap.*"

"I couldn't have said it better myself," and with those words, Vera appeared behind Charles's back and plunged a tranquilizer into his neck, "Next time, make sure not to drop your ammo," Vera added as Charles fell to the floor.

Stepping over Charles's body tentatively, Vera looked down at Atticus with a mixture of weariness and relief; finally allowing her tears to come, she raced to the floor towards him as he held out his arms for her. Finally, Vera felt safe. Atticus just sat on the floor for a while, stunned, holding Vera in his arms. Slowly, but surely, he took out his phone and dialed 911.

"Hello, I'd like to report an attack..."

CHAPTER TWENTY-SEVEN

The police rushed into the school just minutes after Atticus made his phone call. They walked toward Vera and Atticus prepared to question them, but before they could say anything Vera started to speak.

"Our school principal is in his office. He's been sedated with tranquilizers so someone should go check on him right away, he may need medical attention...my attacker is over there on the ground. He's attacked me before. If you check his criminal record it'll show that I have a restraining order against him from about a month ago. If you want I can..."

"Vera," Atticus said kindly, "Let the officers do their thing...try and calm down."

Vera placed her head on Atticus's shoulder and simply replied, "Okay."

Once the officers had inspected the scene they officially began questioning the two teenagers. Vera told them she came into the school to try to talk with Principal McCormac (she left out the why, of course). She told them how Charles had followed her into the school, how Atticus had come to help her when she didn't come back to his party for a while, and how the two had fought Charles off together.

"You two are lucky to be alive; not many people can say that they have friends that would come to their aid like you two did for each other," one of the police officers commented after the questioning, "We're just going to have some paramedics take a look at the two of you. You both looked a little bashed up."

"We called your families," a second police officer added, "They're on their way to pick you both up."

"Vera, you should probably call Rachel...let her know what happened. Let her know that you're okay," Atticus said turning to his friend.

"Yeah, I should...good thinking."

Vera was about to dial Rachel's number when her phone rang. Her grandmother was already calling her. Vera picked up the phone only to hear Rachel's frantic voice.

"Vera, are you okay? I heard your thoughts, but I didn't know where you were or how I could help."

"I'm fine, Rachel. I'll tell you all about it later. Just know I'm fine. Wait, why were you reading my thoughts in the first place?"

"Call it a hunch...I've been checking in on you, well your thoughts, at least once a day anyway."

"Oh...okay," Vera said slightly confused but too tired and stressed to press the matter.

"And Atticus? Is he fine too? I heard his thoughts when they got closer to yours."

"Yes, Atticus is fine too. We're both going to be fine...I'll call you later okay?"

"Okay, Vera. And tell Atticus thank you for me."

"Okay, Rachel, I will. I'll talk to you later, okay?"

"Okay. Oh, Vera?"

"Yeah, Rachel?"

"I love you."

"I love you, too," Vera said with a smile and hung up the phone.

The paramedics arrived almost seconds after Vera finished her phone call. Neither Vera nor Atticus had to go to the hospital, a fact which the both of them were immensely thankful for. The paramedics gave the Walkers specific instructions on what to do with Vera – she had indeed suffered a mild concussion and subsequently, had to be woken up every couple hours during the night to make sure she was okay. She was also told to see a doctor the next day. Atticus had a few cuts that required butterfly bandages but not stitches, and the paramedics set his nose which was deemed to be broken.

Following what seemed to Vera and Atticus to be a sea of questions and inspections, the officers and medical personnel finally left leaving Mr. and Mrs. Wells, Mr. and Mrs. Walker, Benedict, Sebastian, Vera, and Atticus alone to talk and go home.

Mrs. Walker was the first parent to speak once the police departed, "Vera honey, maybe we should take you home. You've had a rough day...some rest would do you some good."

"You should get back too, Atticus," added Mr. Wells seriously, "All of your guests have left and all of us could use some time to calm down."

"Can we get ice cream?" Bastian begged, his question seemingly coming from nowhere, "I'm sure Vera and Atticus would love some ice cream. I always like ice cream when I'm upset and scared..."

"You like ice cream all the time, Bastian," Ben added laughing.

"Well, of course, Ben, but don't you think Finch and Vera could use some sugar? I mean, look at them!"

"They do look pretty terrible. Look at Finch's nose!"

"Thanks a lot, guys," Atticus said mid-laugh.

"We only speak the truth, Finch," Bastian said proudly.

"That you do, boys that you do," said Atticus patting Bastian on the back and laughing.

"All jokes aside, I actually could really go for some Ben & Jerry's, Mom and Dad. Rare as it is that I admit this, the boys have a point," Vera said honestly and slightly amused.

"Dean, are you and Eleanor up for ice cream?" Mr. Walker asked Mr. and Mrs. Wells with a grin.

"I think ice cream would help boost all of our spirits," Mr. Wells replied smiling, "Shall we walk? It's so close we can come get the cars later. Walking might do all of our nerves some good."

"I think a good walk would be nice," Atticus said with a sigh of relief.

And as the two families began to walk towards the ice cream stand, Vera looked up at Atticus.

"Thank you," she said, her voice full of care and appreciation.

"Thank *you*," Atticus replied in a similar tone.

For the first few minutes of the walk, the two teenagers walked separately, until, just before the families reached the ice cream stand, Atticus, without averting his gaze from the road, and while holding his hand out to Vera, said the words she had been wanting him to say for the entire walk.

"Get over here, you losermuffin." And with those words, Vera took his hand smiling, interlacing her fingers with his.

EPILOGUE

The rest of the school year seemed to pass so fast that Vera and Atticus had to struggle to keep up with everything. Between exams, telepathy lessons, and weekly questions from the press, Vera felt as though her brain was going to implode with stress and information, and Atticus was quickly getting tired of the words "no comment". The one silver lining, in Vera's view, was that Charles had been placed in juvenile hall while he was awaiting trial for assault and attempted murder. Even with the advantage of being a minor, his case still didn't look as though it could possibly swing in his favor.

Most of Vera and Atticus's last week of school was spent hanging with Evan, Ashliana, Kyle, and Chelsea, whether it was to study for their finals, spend a day chilling by Lake Champlain, or go out on triple dates. In any case, they didn't care; for Vera and Atticus, their near-death experience made finals look like a walk in the park.

Mid-way through their last day of school, Vera and Atticus were called into Principal McCormac's office for reasons mysterious and unknown to both of them. As soon as they entered the office, the two of them knew something wasn't quite right. Principal McCormac, who normally looked completely at ease, looked overly concerned as he hurriedly locked the door behind them and closed the windows. Then, after doing a quick scan of the room, he began to speak swiftly and intently to both of them.

"I am one of the witnesses for Charles Jenkins's trial. You probably don't know this, but close to the end of your struggle with him in the school, I was awake. I was groggy and lethargic from Charles's tranquilizer, but, though I couldn't move to help you, I still know what I saw. And what I saw was you, Vera, step in front of Atticus when Charles pointed his gun at him. And then I saw Charles slowly backing away, and his face didn't just show sadness, defeat, and remorse...Charles looked confused and terrified even though you were hardly speaking to him. And even though few people during the trial will believe him if he says something strange made him so afraid, those same people, jurors in particular, will want answers."

"Principal McCormac, I..." Vera began before being cut off.

"Vera, I don't need nor want an explanation for what happened because I don't think there is a simple one. All I want to know is what you and Atticus want me to *say you said* during that time when Charles was backing up towards the wall, gun in hand. I need to know what you want me to tell the jury when they ask what words could have scared Charles so much."

"Sir," Atticus began, "You're right...it's not simple. But what can Vera and I tell you that could help with the trial?"

"Atticus, I know how much you care for Vera. I've known for a long time that you would do anything for her. It's because of this that I need you especially to please know I am not your enemy. I truly am trying to help you, but I can't do that unless you give me words. What I saw...I can't explain what I saw and heard that day. I saw a football player-sized teenager back away from a girl half his size in terror while responding to questions and comments that never came out of your mouth, Vera. It was as if he was hearing something that I couldn't hear and Atticus couldn't hear, but for him was very real."

"What are you saying, sir?" Vera asked as a nervous tremor bubbled from her voice.

"I'm saying that...I have always been a man who takes pride in both telling and knowing the truth, but even more than that, I have always been a man who would do close to anything in order to help a cause that I know in my heart to be right, moral, and just. Vera, Atticus...I want to help you, but I can't do that unless you meet me halfway. I don't need to know the whole truth, just enough so that I can understand, beyond any shadow of a doubt, that defending you is what is right, what is moral, and what is just. Do you understand?"

It was in that instant that Vera Walker had an epiphany, and without so much as a moment of hesitation, Vera looked at Atticus with a penetrating stare that emanated trust and understanding, and smiled, and then turned to Principal McCormac before addressing him.

"In the novel *To Kill a Mockingbird*, Atticus Finch says the following to his daughter, Scout, 'You never really understand a person until you consider things from his point of view – until you climb into his skin and walk around in it.' In all the times I have read these words in Harper Lee's novel, I've never truly understood them until these past few months. Maybe that's because I never let myself understand them, or I couldn't let myself understand them because I was too afraid. But one thing I know for sure is that I understand them now, more than ever, and not because of the story I'm about to tell you, the story detailing all the excitement Atticus and I have dealt with over the past months. It's because of what you told me just a few seconds ago, and because of what my grandmother told me about who I am and who I can become. I know that no matter how stupid or jealous or stubborn I may ever get, Atticus will never stop caring for me and seeing the best in me. You see, Principal McCormac, for the first time in my life I'm finally able to look at my life, and the people who share it with me, and see the beautiful truths in it, without tarnishing them with my doubts, skepticism, and fears. And that is so liberating that you may not even be able to begin to imagine how that feels."

And with those words Vera turned back towards Atticus, walked to his side, and grabbed his hand, giving it a knowing squeeze, and then continued talking to Principal McCormac, "My name is Vera Eleanor Walker, but I wasn't always known by this name. I was born Ella Marchmont, daughter of Matthew and Chloe Marchmont, and I am a telepath."

Vera Eleanor Walker didn't know what would come of her telling Principal McCormac about her gift, but oddly enough, as she told him her strange story, her hand still grasping Atticus's, all her feelings of dread and distrust seemed to diminish. Because if Vera had learned anything in the past few months it was that, although evil will always exist and attempt to consume the world in bitterness, hate, and darkness, good will always exist too, and will always be there to battle even the greatest amounts of darkness with courage, loyalty, trust, truth, and love.

Rachel Reilly once said to Vera, "Don't let your inner demons consume you... but rather let yourself be consumed by unseen miracles; let yourself be consumed by beautiful truth." Vera would always be stubborn and outspoken and opinionated, but she knew for sure she would never be completely lost or hopeless or alone as long as she continued to put her faith in the people she loved and the people who loved her in return. And that, Vera thought, was the most beautiful of all of life's truths: one worth trusting and believing.

~ A very special thanks to some of my favorite "losermuffins" ~

- To my family and friends, near and far, for their constant love and support (especially Miss Emily for being my first Young Adult reader ever!)
- To some of my first fans and "extra pairs of eyes" during my final editing stages: the 2015-2016 Mountain View Middle School students in Ms. McCaffrey's and Ms. Varga's Language Arts classes
- To my friend, Chelsea Varga, who loves these characters as much as I do, and who spent countless hours reading and rereading their adventures to help in the editing process

ABOUT THE AUTHOR

 Caela Anne Provost has always been immersed in literature, especially books focused on young adults. She graduated from Marist College in the Honors Program with a bachelor's degree in English and minor in music. She went on to earn her master's degree in English with her thesis paper, "Understanding the Role of the 'Intellectual Girl' in Young Adult Literature: A Discussion of the Portrayal of the Female Protagonists Hermione Granger and Meg Murry."

Provost is passionate about the ability of literature to change a person's life. She works as the North American Officer for University College Cork in Ireland, and she lives in Mine Hill, New Jersey.

Made in the USA
Middletown, DE
21 March 2017